Palgrave Science Fiction and Fantasy: A New Canon

Series Editors
Sean Guynes, Michigan Publishing, University of Michigan–Ann Arbor,
Ann Arbor, USA
Keren Omry, Department of English, University of Haifa, Haifa, Israel

Palgrave Science Fiction and Fantasy: A New Canon provides short introductions to key works of science fiction and fantasy (SFF) speaking to why a text, trilogy, or series matters to SFF as a genre as well as to readers, scholars, and fans. These books aim to serve as a go-to resource for thinking on specific texts and series and for prompting further inquiry. Each book will be less than 30,000 words and structured similarly to facilitate classroom use. Focusing specifically on literature, the books will also address film and TV adaptations of the texts as relevant. Beginning with background and context on the text's place in the field, the author and how this text fits in their oeuvre, and the socio-historical reception of the text, the books will provide an understanding of how students, readers, and scholars can think dynamically about a given text. Each book will describe the major approaches to the text and how the critical engagements with the text have shaped SFF. Engaging with classic works as well as recent books that have been taken up by SFF fans and scholars, the goal of the series is not to be the arbiters of canonical importance, but to show how sustained critical analysis of these texts might bring about a new canon. In addition to their suitability for undergraduate courses, the books will appeal to fans of SFF.

More information about this series at
https://link.springer.com/bookseries/16580

D. Harlan Wilson

Alfred Bester's *The Stars My Destination*

A Critical Companion

D. Harlan Wilson
Wright State University-Lake Campus
Celina, OH, USA

ISSN 2662-8562 ISSN 2662-8570 (electronic)
Palgrave Science Fiction and Fantasy: A New Canon
ISBN 978-3-030-96945-5 ISBN 978-3-030-96946-2 (eBook)
https://doi.org/10.1007/978-3-030-96946-2

Cover illustration: Pattern © John Rawsterne/patternhead.com

This Palgrave Macmillan imprint is published by the registered company Springer Nature Switzerland AG
The registered company address is: Gewerbestrasse 11, 6330 Cham, Switzerland

Series Editors' Preface

The infinite worlds of science fiction and fantasy (SFF) dance along the borders between the possible and the impossible, the familiar and the strange, the immediate and the ever-approaching horizon. Speculative fiction in all its forms has been considered a genre, a medium, a mode, a practice, a compilation of themes, or a web of assertions. With this in mind, *Palgrave Science Fiction and Fantasy: A New Canon* offers an expansive and dynamic approach to thinking SFF, destabilizing notions of *the* canon, so long associated with privilege, power, class, and hegemony. We take canon not as a singular and unchallenged authority but as shifting and thoughtful consensus among an always-growing collective of readers, scholars, and writers.

The cultural practice and production of speculation has encompassed novels, stories, plays, games, music, comics, and other media, with a lineage dating back at least to the nineteenth-century precursors through to the most recent publications. Existing scholarship has considered some of these media extensively, often with particular focus on film and TV. It is for this reason that *Palgrave Science Fiction and Fantasy* will forgo the cinematic and televisual, aspiring to direct critical attention at the other nodes of SFF expression.

Each volume in the series introduces, contextualizes, and analyzes a single work of SFF that ranges from the acknowledged "classic" to the should-be-classic, and asks two basic, but provocative, questions: *Why does this text matter to SFF?* and *Why does (or should) this text matter to SFF readers, scholars, and fans?* Thus, the series joins into conversation both with scholars and students of the field to examine the parameters of SFF studies and the changing valences of fundamental categories like genre, medium, and canon. By emphasizing the critical approaches and major questions each text inspires, the series aims to offer "go-to" books for thinking about, writing on, and teaching major works of SFF.

Ann Arbor, USA   Sean Guynes
Haifa, Israel   Keren Omry

Praise for *Alfred Bester's* The Stars My Destination

"This monograph demonstrates several reasons why Alfred Bester's *The Stars My Destination* remains one of the most fascinating SF novels ever, even 65 years after it was first published. There are, for example, the book's 'proto-cyberpunk style' and 'pyrotechnic' plot, its strange anti-hero, Gully Foyle, its connections to other works, including *Frankenstein*, its representation of a twenty-fifth century society that often seems all too familiar, and its essential plot element, the transformation of Bester's 'stereotype Common Man' into a Promethean figure at the novel's end. For anyone interested in Alfred Bester, Wilson's book is essential reading."

—Patrick A. McCarthy, Professor of English, University of Miami, USA, and author of *The Riddles of Finnegans Wake* (1980)

"Alfred Bester was essentially writing parody during his great period, parody of a field he loved for the very contempt it was able to instill and extract from him. It was the junkiness of science fiction which enthralled him—his stories and his two great novels bestow the armament of junk upon narrative. In this dazzling study of *The Stars My Destination*, D. Harlan Wilson shows us how Bester took the eviscerated, glowing heart of the artichoke and pronounced it as torn from heaven."

—Barry N. Malzberg, author of *Beyond Apollo* (1972) and *Galaxies* (1975)

"D. Harlan Wilson's study is the perfect example of how rigorous literary scholarship can shine a light on a forgotten text and really put it front and center for a contemporary readership. Connecting Alfred Bester's experimental novel of the 1950s through intertextual lines, Wilson uncovers the rhizome that is the SF megatext: from monomyth to mad scientist, from *Frankenstein* to *Neuromancer*, from Joyce's modernism to Wells' scientific romances, from proto-SF to cyberpunk. And the best thing is that Wilson remains true to his subject of study, mirroring Bester's 'pyrotechnic' style in his scholarship. This monograph is a rush of densely packed readings and analyses, giving the story of Gully Foyle its due in the history of science fiction, and revealing its contemporary importance."

—Lars Schmeink, Liverhulme Visiting Professor, University of Leeds, UK, and author of *Biopunk Dystopias: Genetic Engineering, Society, and Science Fiction* (2016)

CONTENTS

About the Author

D. Harlan Wilson is an American novelist, playwright, editor, critic, and college professor. He is the author of over 30 book-length works of fiction and nonfiction, many of which have won literary awards, and hundreds of his essays, reviews, and stories have appeared in journals, magazines, and anthologies across the world in multiple languages. Website: dharlanwilson.com. Twitter & Instagram: @DHarlanWilson.

CHAPTER 1

Introduction

Abstract Alfred Bester's *The Stars My Destination* is a proto-cyberpunk novel that shares common ground with Marshall McLuhan's media theories and represents an increasingly technological society. Bester's desire to become a Renaissance Man in his youth informed his authorship and led to a deep resentment for other SF authors, who he blamed for the genre's inability to transcend its pulp roots and boyish inclinations. Propelled by its Hugo Award-winning predecessor *The Demolished Man*, *Stars* charted new literary terrain and inspired SF's most innovative movements: the New Wave (1960s and 1970s) and cyberpunk (1980s). The latter movement was the genre's death knell as the futuristic technologies depicted in its narratives bled into the real world and rendered SF a twentieth-century artifact.

Keywords Bester · Biography · Sci-fi · Media · Technology

Hammers of Demolition and Redemption

Midway through the twentieth century, Marshall McLuhan published his first book, *The Mechanical Bride: Folklore of Industrial Man* (1951), a study of the American culture industry that explores the effects of popular

D. Harlan Wilson, *Alfred Bester's The Stars My Destination*,
Palgrave Science Fiction and Fantasy: A New Canon,
https://doi.org/10.1007/978-3-030-96946-2_1

media. Many reviewers were confused by McLuhan's rhizomatic method as much as the subject matter, which had never been probed with such bravura. Five years later, UK publisher Sidgwick and Jackson released Alfred Bester's *Tiger! Tiger!* (1956). The novel was renamed *The Stars My Destination* in 1957 by its US publisher, Signet Books. Like McLuhan, Bester hurled readers into a vortex of wonder, spectacle, and technology that was at once familiar and estranging, transcendent and disarming, preposterous and perfectly (in)sane.

Bester and McLuhan were proto-cyberpunks who paved the way for late capitalist SF and media culture in the twentieth century. The cyberpunk movement of the 1980s can be directly traced back to fictional and theoretical works by both authors. To a certain extent, *Stars* takes the baton from *The Mechanical Bride* and runs with it. There is no evidence that Bester read McLuhan before composing his novel. Stylistically and thematically, however, they exhibit ripe similarities in the form of quixotic approaches to narrative, representations of the anxiety and agency induced by the cultural maelstrom, and an attention to the vicissitudes of corporate power, patriarchy, and abuse—all cyberpunk staples. Most importantly, both texts point toward a future distinguished by *the science fictionalization of reality*. This, of course, is the future that has overtaken us. McLuhan predicted the wave. Bester and his cyberpunk descendants rode the wave. And now here we are, crashed on the Terminal Beach.

A collection of "exhibits," *The Mechanical Bride* is a "Frankenstein fantasy" that concerns the "widely occurring cluster image of sex, technology, and death" in consumer-capitalist culture, especially advertising (McLuhan, *Mechanical* 29). McLuhan adopts a high-energy, immersive, and oblique style, compelling readers to make their own connections and dynamically engage with the material. Style is a way of seeing, just as it is for cyberpunk's foundational texts: Ridley Scott's *Blade Runner* (1981) and William Gibson's *Neuromancer* (1984). Bester does likewise in *Stars*, challenging readers to manage their expectations, pushing the limits of the SF genre, and manifesting a pyrotechnic style that reifies his content and characters.

The monster of culture is the apple of McLuhan's eye. Bester has his eye on this apple, too, but the twenty-fifth century depicted in *Stars* is a virtual circus of monsters. One monster, however, towers above all the rest: Gully Foyle.

Bester's quintessential antihero is one of the most complex, thought-provoking, and problematic ever created in SF, pieced together with the scraps of protagonists from earlier literary works, and enhanced by Bester's own authorial mad scientism. Foyle's degradation is the product of social and cultural forces, and his struggle to find and assert his identity bears with it the litany of violence endemic to all quests for self-identification. He is a technologized tiger who channels the darkest essences of McLuhan's mechanical bride. When we meet him in the first chapter, this "stereotype Common Man" has been left for dead (*Stars* 17). As the novel progresses, we watch him transform into a superman, an "infernal machine" (23), ultimately "the archetypal Besterman," which Peter Nicholls describes as "the 200th-century, pulp equivalent of the malcontent of Jacobean revenge dramas, brooding, sardonic, obsessed and murderous—at once ironic commentator and brutal actor in a dark, amoral world" ("Alfred"). In essence, the Besterman is the Batman. Demonic angel, angelic demon—either hybrid will do. It's no coincidence that Batman's co-creator, Bill Finger, taught Bester how to write comics. The Besterman needs the Fall as much as the Rise; his superheroic pathology depends upon the hammers of demolition and redemption.

In his most renowned book, *Understanding Media: The Extensions of Man* (1964), McLuhan builds upon *The Mechanical Bride*. He hypothesizes that all technologies amplify the body, ranging from low tech like speech (i.e., *uttering* equals *outering*) and clothing ("our extended skin") to high tech like computers, robots, and nukes. These amplifications enhance us, but they also amputate us, as every form of newness can only be brought to bear by relegating that from which it sprung. "Any invention or technology is an extension or self-amputation of our physical bodies, and such extension also demands new ratios or new equilibriums among the other organs and extensions of the body" (McLuhan, *Understanding* 67). Foyle himself becomes an amplified amputation when he refurbishes his body and cybernetically extends himself through alterego Geoffrey Fourmyle of Ceres, "the classic *bourgeois gentilhomme*, the upstart *nouveau riche* of all time" (*Stars* 124). This extension relegates the gutter-dwelling prole he used to be, but the ghost of that prole continues to haunt him like a phantom limb. He is amplified/amputated by class as well as technology, two of cyberpunk's most prevalent tropes.

In the end, Foyle/Fourmyle *foils* the SF heroes that preceded him and charts new terrain for the tigers that followed in his wake. The animal is an evocative signifier that goes far beyond the Māori mask tattooed onto his face and the poem from which Bester borrowed his original title and dominant themes, William Blake's "The Tyger" (1794). More than anything, it represents Bester's rancorous artistry and the hunger to carve out his own unique niche in a literary wilderness that he perceived to be largely stagnant, lackluster, and redundant. As an author, Bester is as much a tiger as his Ahabesque monomaniac. "I HATE science fiction for what it has been," he wrote in 1953. "I love it for what it will be" ("Trematode" 11). He thought SF was capable of much more than the status quo it chronically delivered, and *Stars* pointed the way for the most inventive and stylish narratives that the genre would ever see. According to Paul Williams, the novel's "first publication in 1956 was a major event in the history of contemporary science fiction" (v).

Renaissance Man: Biography

Alfred Morton Bester was born on December 18, 1913, in Manhattan, New York City; he died in Doylestown, Pennsylvania, in 1987 of complications from a broken hip. Isaac Asimov once said that he never heard his friends call him anything but "Alfie" ("In Memoriam" 25). I only know as much about his private, day-to-day life as what I've read in interviews, articles, and personal accounts by other authors, but I get the sense that he lived as hard as he wrote, propelled by the same intensity that informs his novels and stories. Tellingly, he left his literary estate to his bartender.

Bester's well-documented desire to become a Renaissance man dates back to his early life. As a child and college student, his imagination conjured one future occupation and identity after another. He even referred to himself as a "Renaissance kid" (Bishop 24), but he lacked the gumption and follow-through to manifest any of his self-extrapolations, which eventually led him to SF. In addition to a scientist, a chess player, an artist, and an astronomer, "I wanted to be a physician, an adventurer, a fullback, a composer […] and never became them because the reality of accomplishment was so much less glamorous than the dreams. And I was so naturally led to science-fiction, for that form of literature provided me with the fulfillment of my dreams at no more cost than a pleasant hour's reading" (Bester, "Trematode" 11–12). Like so many readers and writers, SF was an escape pod from the monotony of real life. In due course, Bester would aspire to make that pod his own, pushing the genre in new directions.

Predictably, Bester's Bestermen tend to be Renaissance men. Gully is the touchstone, as he indicates in the guise of Fourmyle of Ceres: "I dance, speak four languages miserably, study science and philosophy, write pitiful poetry, blow myself up with idiotic experiments, fence like a fool, box like a buffoon" (*Stars* 169). Again and again, this driven, charismatic author's penchant for self-diversity (and self-effacement) bled into his characters.

As an SF writer, Bester started in the pulps and ended as a Grand Master. Along the way, his early obsession with "the ideal of the Renaissance Man" led him elsewhere ("Science Fiction" 409). He became a writer by trade and by name—a "working stiff," he frequently called himself—but he didn't limit himself to one form or genre of writing. He pursued multiple avenues of expression within his chosen profession, personifying the diversity and well-roundedness after which he pined during boyhood. As Jad Smith foregrounds in his biocritical study of Bester's life and work, "He focused on SF only intermittently during his nearly fifty years as a professional writer and, at times, maintained few ties with the field" (2).

Bester was a furious self-critic. In "Science Fiction and the Renaissance Man," he denigrates his juvenilia, saying he sold "half a dozen miserable stories by the grace of two kindly editors at Standard Magazines who enjoyed discussing James Joyce with me and bought my stories out of pity" before his polymathic impulse led him to comics (410). All told, he sold over a dozen stories between 1939 and 1942, punctuated by the novelette "Hell Is Forever," whose byzantine, multigeneric style prefigures *Stars*. He didn't publish another SF story for nearly a decade. In the interim, he worked in radio, television, and comics, all of which contributed to the evolution of his style. Comics in particular "gave me an ample opportunity to get a lot of lousy writing out of my system" ("My Affair" 453), but it also contributed to his signature prose. Distinguished by aggressive bricolage, meta-playfulness, overcoding, visual dynamism, and compulsive fever pitches, the epitome of this prose can be found in *Stars*, a novel for whom the pyrotechnic label is richly deserved, if not definitive. Smith synthesizes the impact of Bester's experience working in other media: "He brought valuable skills with him from comics, radio, and television—including a highly developed sense of pacing, a flair for both comic and hard-boiled dialogue, and a strongly visual approach to narrative—and he combined them with his own freewheeling imagination. To boot, he had a hip, iconoclastic New York attitude" (3).

Ennui is any Renaissance man or woman's worst enemy; nothing cripples him or her like boredom and the anvil of stagnation. Bester grew weary with commercial writing and returned to SF in a consummate pursuit of newness. While it would prove to be more limiting than liberating for him, he believed that, at its core, SF's potential for genuine innovation and creative breakthroughs surpassed all other genres. Unfortunately, he discovered that SF publishers, editors, and authors rarely tapped and harnessed the core's energy.

In the 1950s and early 1960s, Bester came into his own. He sold his most enduring stories, among them "Fondly Fahrenheit" (1954), a tale about a wealthy playboy and his murderous android doppelgänger that extrapolates John Steinbeck's *Of Mice and Men* (1937) and, like *Stars*, Mary Shelley's *Frankenstein* (1818). He also produced two of SF's most significant, influential novels of the post-WW2 era. His first novel, *The Demolished Man*, won the first annual Hugo Award in 1953. In the imagined future of this SF noir, telepathy has become normative and murder is virtually nonexistent—"Espers" or "peepers" can detect a crime before it happens or finger a perpetrator after the fact. The plot involves a schizophrenic, megalomaniacal industrialist, Ben Reich, who commits murder and attempts to evade the long, telepathic arm of the law. In the end, police detective Lincoln Powell apprehends him and Reich must undergo Demolition, a process that will recondition his psychological flows and turn him from a minus man into a "plus value" (242).

Bester loved Freud and often injected psychoanalytic ideas into his fiction. Reich is a Freudian case study amplified by Gully Foyle, a latent übermensch on the precipice of greatness. A Nietzschean venom flows through the veins of both Bestermen, although Foyle's Zarathustra packs a harder punch than Reich's. So does *Stars* elevate *Demolished* in terms of world-building, visual intricacy, the vagaries of inner space, and "special effects." The release of the novel in 1956 solidified Bester's status as an SF prizefighter. Several years later, however, he would depart from the genre again, partly because of a slow-burning antipathy for the way SF was being written, mostly because he took a full-time job at the travel magazine *Holiday* as a writer and editor. "An exciting new writing life began for me," Bester wrote in 1975. "I was no longer immured in my workshop; I was getting out and interviewing interesting people in interesting professions. Reality had become so colorful for me that I no longer needed the therapy of science fiction. And since the magazine imposed no constraints on me, outside of the practical requirements of professional magazine technique, I no longer needed a safety valve" ("My Affair" 472).

His tenure at *Holiday* lasted until 1970 when the magazine down-sized and relocated from New York to Indiana. During this period, Bester published a few stories, but for the most part he was AWOL from SF … until he made a concerted effort to return to "his first love" a second time with "The Animal Fair," a morality "play" on George Orwell's *Animal Farm* (1945) that appeared in the October 1972 issue of *The Magazine of Fantasy and Science Fiction* (473). The previous decade had seen him badmouth SF with impunity—even while serving as reviews editor of *F&SF*—but the birthright of his two great SF novels had grown more powerful than Bester's best efforts to piss everybody off, and he was welcomed back to the genre, especially by authors and editors affiliated with the New Wave movement, which was at its height in the early 70s. This final stage of his career included his most experimental SF novels: *The Computer Connection* (1975), *Golem^{100}* (1980), and *The Deceivers* (1981). None of them came close to generating the buzz and acclaim of *Stars* or *Demolished*, and whereas Bester contended that *Golem^{100}* was "beyond a doubt" his best book (qtd. in Bishop 23), they were all widely criticized for a variety of reasons, above all authorial self-indulgence and complicated plotlines. In fact, these later novels are each underrated in their own right. Readers came down on them because what they really wanted was a repackaging of *Demolished* and *Stars*. But the Renaissance itch followed Bester to the end of his life, shirking redundancy and compelling him to make new doorways in the drywall.

Bester had been slated to be the Guest of Honor at WorldCon in 1987, but he couldn't attend because of his hip injury. He died the same year after learning that he would be the 1988 Nebula Grand Master, an annual title bestowed by the Science Fiction and Fantasy Writers of America. Fiona Kelleghan nicely condenses his legacy: "Bester, like Gully a delighter in fire, fights, and rebellion, hurled himself into the unknown like a burning spear. Due to his ambition, skill, and wild talent, science fiction was thrust boldly forward through an innovative, enduring work of the imagination" (1273).

Critique of Science Fiction

Like a play or movie, Bester's SF career can be broken into three acts with two intermissions that lasted about a decade apiece, one in the 1940s, the other in the 1960s. In the first act (1930s), he gained footing and tried to find his voice. He flourished in the second act (1950s), becoming a star.

The third act (1970s) was mostly afterburn, but again, his later novels and stories deserve more attention and applause than they have received, if only because of his undying resolve to compose original works of art and literature that subverted the norm.

Bester's critique of SF ebbed and flowed throughout his lifetime. It reached a crescendo in the second act. He didn't suffer fools easily, and if he smelled bullshit, he called it out with a megaphone. His first and only encounter with renowned editor John W. Campbell, Jr. in 1950 clinched his irritation and dissatisfaction. He admired what Campbell had done for the genre, forsaking the boyish adventures of pulp SF for more sophisticated, adult themes. When Bester met him in person to discuss revisions to "Oddy and Id" (1950) for publication in *Astounding*, however, Campbell alienated him with his personality as much as his principles and editorial ideas. The encounter "solidified his conception of himself as a writer standing 'outside' the SF world, looking in" (Smith 85).

Hungry for literary acclaim, Philip K. Dick famously tried to break into the mainstream and leave SF in his dust, producing nine non-SF novels. Bester, too, wanted to be respected as a literary author and aspired for mass appeal. Even after the success of *Demolition* and *Stars*, he always felt like an amateur SF author, and he "was convinced that his talents lay in the mainstream writing field, though he would not make much headway" (Raucci 9). His most pointed effort, the posthumously published *Tender Loving Rage* (1991), was rejected by every publisher that read it during his lifetime. Bester belonged in SF, as did Dick; no other genre harbored such imaginative promise, and they were both great at writing it. Curiously, SF's practitioners were relatively conservative and adhered to a strict code of conduct, believing that the literature needed to be written a certain way for a certain type of reader. Bester hated this grossly ironic limitation.

If Bester had his way, SF would be as he described it in "Science Fiction and the Renaissance Man," "far above the utilitarian yardsticks of the technical minds, the agency minds, the teaching minds. Science fiction is not for Squares. It's for the modern Renaissance Man … vigorous, versatile, zestful … full of romantic curiosity and impractical speculation" (422). In this essay and others, he rants and raves about how the genre consistently fails to manifest his ideal, pulling no punches and mincing no words. Of course, there are exceptions, most of which he itemizes in "The Perfect Composite Science Fiction Author." Among them are Robert Heinlein, the "Big Daddy," "Old Pro," and "Kipling" of the genre (436);

Theodore Sturgeon, "the most perceptive, the most sensitive, and the most adult of science fiction writers" (437); Robert Sheckley, "possibly the most polished" SF author (438); James Blish, "a dedicated craftsman with a deep philosophical bias" (438); Isaac Asimov, whose "encyclopedic enthusiasm" distinguishes him from the horde (442); Philip Jose Farmer, "possibly the only author who genuinely, with discipline, extrapolates" (440); and Ray Bradbury, SF's preeminent stylist (442). At the same time, Bester has plenty of bad things to say about these "exceptions," regretting, for example, that Asimov's "greatest story was his first," and he even argues that Asimov "is not a real fiction writer" (439). In short, Bester had problems with everybody, including himself, although self-effacement took a back seat to disparaging the genre and its people as a whole.

To say the least, Bester's authorial persona belonged to a curmudgeon, despite the inherent performativity of his antagonism. Clearly, he wanted to incite a reaction, but that didn't mean he was wrong. In "A Diatribe Against Science Fiction," he blames authors, repeatedly stating that they are "killing" the genre. This article appeared in 1961 and vexed more than a few of his peers. Bester uses the royal "we" in the thrust of his attack:

> Almost everybody agrees that science fiction has fallen upon hard times—too many bad books and too few good books are being published today—and many people want to know why. Publishers, editors, and the public have been blamed. We disagree. We think authors are responsible. The average quality of writing in the field today is extraordinarily low. We don't speak of style; it's astonishing how well amateurs and professionals alike can handle words. […] No, we speak of content; of the thought, theme, and drama of the stories, which reflect the author himself. Many practicing science fiction authors reveal themselves in their works as very small people, disinterested in reality, inexperienced in life, incapable of relating science fiction to human beings, and withdrawing from the complexities of living into their make-believe worlds. […] Their science is a mere repetition of what has been done before. They ring minuscule changes on played-out themes, concepts which were established and exhausted a decade ago. They play with odds and ends and left-overs. In past years this has had a paralyzing effect on their technique. (431–32)

As if these one-two punches aren't enough, Bester concludes with a forceful uppercut, denouncing the character of SF authors, "empty people who have failed as human beings. As a class they are lazy, irresponsible, immature. They are incapable of producing contemporary fiction because they know nothing about life, cannot reflect life, and have no adult comment to make about life. They are silly childish people who have taken refuge in science fiction where they can establish their own arbitrary rules about reality to suit their own inadequacy. And like most neurotics, they cherish the delusion that they're 'special'" (434).

No matter how hard he tried, Bester couldn't knock out his opponent. To this day, nearly every professional SF author still writes prescribed formulas for SF editors who still want a very specific type of canned writing. These are the authors and editors who purport to be on the cutting edge of imagination and narrative. But we're assuming that the SF genre still exists. I would argue that it is largely a twentieth-century phenomenon. In the last two decades, reality has effectively absorbed and digested SF (or vice versa) like a phagocyte.

There were really only two short periods where SF made genuinely innovative strides with the New Wave and cyberpunk movements, upshots of the evolving media environment and the postwar explosion of electric technologies. Bester was an icon for both movements. He wasn't alone in his contention that SF needed improvement. Barry N. Malzberg, for instance, was another uncompromising livewire associated with the New Wave who seared the genre in scores of articles and meta-SF novels. But Bester has certainly been one of the most outspoken SF critics, and it's a big part of his legacy. He foresaw the death of SF long before it fell to its knees and toppled into the dirt.

THE CLASSIC PYROTECHNIC NOVEL

Near the end of his career's first act, Bester sold "The Unseen Blushers" (1942) to *Astonishing Stories*. This satirical roman à clef falls into the same territory as *A Moveable Feast* (1964), in which Ernest Hemingway lightly roasts modernist contemporaries like Gertrude Stein, F. Scott Fitzgerald, Ezra Pound, and others. Bester's victims included pulp-SF veterans who he met through his agent, such as Henry Kuttner, Otto Binder, Malcolm Jameson, and Manly Wade Wellman. He was still a young author at this point, but he didn't hesitate to depict his SF contemporaries as a bunch of hacks. Even digs of this nature weren't enough to get the monkey of SF off of his back (the more I read his SF diatribes, veiled or unbound, the more Bester comes off as an addict trying to quit a drug). Granted, the two intermissions between acts gave people time to cool off, but following the indisputable success of *Demolished* and *Stars*, Bester could burn bridges until he was blue in the face. The writing in these novels was too good to let the author's rancor and angst get in the way of how they elevated the genre, captivating readers and setting a new standard for authors.

Bester's library includes over fifty short stories and eight novels, two posthumously published, with the last one, *Psychoshop* (1998), finished by Robert Zelazny. Collectively, his fiction has been referred to as "pyrotechnic," a catchword that has fallen out of vogue but used to be more critically fashionable. Williams says that a pyrotechnic novel

> may be defined as one constructed quite literally like a string of firecrackers, each firecracker igniting the next, each explosion necessarily bigger than the last in order to sustain the impact on the reader. Such a novel, when done well, totally exhausts its reader with its astonishing pace of ideas and events, yet is so gripping that the reader must go on reading in spite of his own exhaustion, triggering a sort of intellectual overdrive, a surge of adrenalin that replaces exhaustion with a state of super-awareness. The breathless conclusion of a pyrotechnic novel leaves the reader certain that more things have happened to him than his dazed mind will ever be able to comprehend or remember. (v–vi)

This type of writing distinguishes most of Bester's novels and many of his stories. Williams argues that *Stars* epitomizes the form, serving as a model for subsequent pyrotechnic novels like Kurt Vonnegut, Jr.'s *The Sirens of Titan* (1959) and Dick's *The Three Stigmata of Palmer Eldritch* (1964).

According to how he describes his writing process, Bester even seems to compose fiction in a pyrotechnic way. "I write out of fever," he claimed in a 1976 reflection on "Fondly Fahrenheit." "I cannot write anything until I'm so saturated with it, bursting with it, that it must come out or I will have no rest" ("Comment" 66). Ruminating on the composition of *Stars*, he has also said: "I write out of hysteria" ("My Affair" 468). This modus resonates in his prose like an atomic ring of fire, and *Stars* might be SF's pyrotechnic masterwork, if not an ur-text for post-*Stars* literature.

Carolyn Wendell defines Bester's style in greater detail: "Reading Bester can be like looking at a firework pinwheel: constant activity, sparks shooting off in every direction, speed, vibrant color and image—and a feeling of losing one's breath" (15). The way he embroiders and unfolds storylines is equally charismatic as well as filmic. "His plots are always scenic, with rapid changes of setting and character occurring every few pages, not unlike cinematic technique. [The] reader is pushed along the inevitable path to a solution at its end. [...] It is this pinwheel effect that has resulted in 'pyrotechnic' evolving as the favorite critical word for Bester. Unfortunately, the first does get out of control at time, and logic and sense are sacrificed for speed and dizzyingly vivid image" (ibid.).

Like Wendell, some readers were put off by Bester's decidedly aggressive prose in novels like *The Computer Connection* and *Golem*[100], both of which turn up the pyrotechnic dial to 11 while lacking the coherence of *Demolished* and *Stars*. Wendell takes issue with *The Computer Connection*, calling it Bester's worst novel for this very reason. "It embodies his worst flaws as a writer and, as such, it probably is most interesting as a study of excessive style. Those techniques which worked before [...]—the rapid scene shifts, the detailed plot, the piling on of image—are here [...] in excess. Those qualities which made his two earlier novels classics make this novel a failure" (40). This stance says more about the failings of Wendell and readers than Bester, who was always trying to do new things. Readers hardly ever want new things, even if they say they do. They want the same things over and over with new, relatively inconspicuous frills. Bester's lifelong struggle against SF has a lot to do with this default infirmity.

Some readers also grimaced at *Star*'s pyrotechnics. While Wendell thinks Bester periodically lost control of his novel, Jesse Bier thinks it's a big-headed mess:

> Bester's style and conception get utterly away from him, virtually out of control. Style never has been one of science fiction's distinctions but, in any case, too many science fictioners, Bester included, forsake the neutral non-distracting style that is probably the best and canniest mode they can hope for. Instead, they offer an unrelenting meretriciousness. Bester, for instance, cannot resist those punningly derivative names, like Gully Foyle and Presteign, and then adds nervous whimsicalities, like "Robin Wednesday." More damagingly, he is at the end of the whole class in showing off a sort of portentous wisdom, usually in the course of greatly increased action and thematic pressure—as if it were a sort of compensatory mechanism. (605)

Bier gets Robin's surname wrong—it's Wednesbury—but he makes his point clear: *Stars* is flawed by over-the-top ornamentation. Understandably, *Demolished* has not been disparaged for alleged superfluities. In retrospect, it is a prototype or template for *Stars*, which amplifies the pyrotechnic apparatus that Bester introduced in his award-winning first novel.

This brings me back to McLuhan's theory that amplification is also amputation, that any technological advancement or gain is necessarily accompanied by a technological falling-off or loss. In the case of *Stars*, readers like Bier felt that Bester sacrificed basic narrative construction for high-octane antics. In fact, *Stars* is the mature, adult version of the comparatively adolescent *Demolished*, as more astute readers grasped. "Though it has the pace and some of the colour of his other book," says Charles Platt, *Demolished* "is never quite as successful, as imaginative, or as satisfying, and the 'open' mystery format must take some of the blame. The plot relies heavily on psychology which is disappointingly glib and shallow" (215). Bester didn't completely excise psychology from *Stars*; rather, he wove psychological principles into the fabric of the narrative so that they didn't glint and stick out. Smith adds: "*Stars* remained fresh and relevant long after its initial publication, while *Demolished*'s Freudian references made it date more quickly. By the early 1970s, the former would be praised as the 'best science fiction of its kind ever written,' the latter viewed as a 'tour de force' marred by its 'formal approach' to psychology" (144).

Additionally, there is a marked difference between each novel's Besterman. Both are hysteric, obsessive-compulsive, schizophrenic monsters, but Gully Foyle is far more dynamic and complex than Ben Reich, and whereas Foyle proves to be a fluid character who evolves and adapts to his surroundings, Reich is comparatively static. In more general terms, Jane Hipolito and Willis E. McNelly assert that, in *Stars*, "Bester's chief concern is to develop what is only implicit in *The Demolished Man*" (78). *Demolished* may have won the Hugo Award, but *Stars* is the superior work as a source of entertainment, an artistic endeavor, and a site for scholarly research.

CONTEXT, COMPOSITION, AND RECEPTION

"The *reclamé* of [*Demolished*] turned me into a science fiction somebody," Bester recounted in 1975, "and people were curious about me" ("My Affair" 467). He went on to write a mainstream novel about his experiences in television, *Who He?* (1953), which turned a decent profit and gave him and his wife Rolly, a radio and Broadway actress, some financial padding. They moved to England in May 1954 and he started research for *Stars*. The idea of writing a novel abroad excited him, but he found it more troublesome than he had planned on. "Everything seemed to go wrong," he said, ranging from his unfamiliarity with English type-writers and manuscript paper to the cold weather that depressed him (468). It wasn't until he and Rolly relocated to Rome in November that Bester finally hit his stride after starting the novel over three times.

In the twenty-first century, we take for granted how easy it is to access information. I haven't been to a library in years—all of my research for this monograph was conducted online with books, maga-zines, articles, and stories downloaded onto my computer, sent to me from Ohio libraries, or purchased from eBay and Amazon—but in the twentieth century, research often required considerable time, travel, and endurance. In Italy, Bester used the British Consulate library to great effect. He still had difficulty finding up-to-date publications about scien-tific developments, so he relied on American editor Tony Boucher and German-American science writer Willy Ley, "plaguing" them with letters (470). He also consulted research materials from his early SF stories. The idea for the Māori tattoo on Gully's face, for example, derived from an anecdote he came across while writing for *South Sea Stories* in the 1930s. The anecdote "was about an English remittance man who landed on one of the islands and wanted to marry a native girl. He had to go through all the native customs, which included tattooing his face. Then, he got the message that he was next in line to inherit a fortune; everyone else had died, and he had to return to England. He couldn't go back with the tattoo on his face, so he had it removed. As he was being rowed out to the sailing ship to take him away, he saw the girl that he married embracing another guy, and got furious, and the scars of the tattooing showed up on his face" (Bester, "Alfred" 35).

Bester finished *Stars* in early 1955, three months after moving to Rome. One of his biggest hurdles had been formulating a viable conclu-sion. "I didn't have a fiery finish in mind. I must have an attack and a finale. I'm like the old Hollywood gag, 'Start with an earthquake and build to a climax'" ("My Affair" 469). A dispute over serialization rights between *Galaxy* and *Fantasy and Science Fiction* in 1956 held up publication in the US. The hardcover edition that was published in the UK as *Tiger! Tiger!* came out in June. Reviewers loved it. In *New Worlds*, Leslie Flood referred to it as a masterpiece that "must surely take its place among the top ten science-fiction novels of all time" (128); Bester, she emphasized, "had resolved to write *the* science-fiction novel to end all such novels" (126).

When it was finally published as *The Stars My Destination* in the US, the novel had already generated considerable buzz. It received a fair share of praise, but there were more mixed feelings among American reviewers. In *Astounding*, P. Schuyler Miller said he liked *Demolished* better and criticized Bester for faulty science. In *Fantastic Universe*, Stefan Santesson reviled it for "violence (or rather blind, dogged hate), plus basic English, plus sex and deliberately exaggerated characterizations. While this obviously has commercial possibilities, is all this an admissible substitute for plotting in the classic sense of that much abused word?" (113). Ten years later in 1967, Damon Knight bashed *Stars* in the second edition of *In Search of Wonder*, calling the characters "not characters but funny hats" (234) and accusing Bester of "bad taste, inconsistency, irrationality, and downright factual errors" (235). Such puritan sentiments, however, invariably included disclaimers. Santesson couldn't deny Bester's innovations, and Miller wondered why a hardcover edition hadn't been published in the US. Even Knight confessed that many of Bester's ideas were "good as gold" and referred to *Stars* as a "work of art" (235, 236).

No work of art is without flaws, and *Stars* is hardly perfect. Bester's representation of patriarchal entitlement and toxic masculinity leaves much to be desired in spite of the author's best satirical, meta-referential efforts. Personally, I'm not a fan of Bester's dialogue; even in its historical context, it sounds affected and clunky to me, like most pulp SF. But it's impossible to deny the overall accomplishment of this singular novel. Contemporary readers, editors, and authors alike habitually treat it with reverence. Authors are outspoken about their feelings, acknowledging the imaginative debt they owe to *Stars*—William Gibson, Samuel R. Delany, Neil Gaiman, Joe Haldeman, Carl Sagan, Isaac Asimov, Spider Robinson, Robert Silverberg, K.W. Jeter, Norman Spinrad, Barry N. Malzberg, Harlan Ellison, M. John Harrison, and Bruce Sterling have all showered the novel with praise. It's almost as if Bester has become a sacrament whose reception must be enunciated to validate one's own SF authorship and alliance. If nothing else, any SF writer or scholar would be remiss without a concerted knowledge of Bester's contribution to the genre. Delany puts it mildly but hits the mark: "Bester is easily the SF writer who brought expertise to its full fruition" (19).

More than the novel's gleeful immorality, the negative feedback that *Stars* received in the 1950s mainly related to Bester's pseudoscientific applications and unrealistic portrayals. Bester devalued science. In his view, the science of SF was altogether subsidiary to characterization. "In a question-answer session at Seacon, 1979, Bester said: 'I *hate* hard science fiction' and went on to explain that he is not even faintly interested in science fact and formula and will happily make it up as he goes along; his concern is people, and the science, valid or invalid, is a mere convenience to place people into stress situations" (Wendell 16). Critics like Knight accused *Stars* of cartoon characters and cirque-du-soleil landscapes that disrupt narrative verisimilitude. Bester didn't care. For him, SF had "taken refuge in science to the detriment of its fiction. In the past this was no problem. The field had the charm of novelty. There were so many fascinating physical avenues to explore—space, time, dimensions, environments—that there was no need for understanding and development of human character. Unfortunately, the novelty is fading today and there is a rising demand for mature character handling" ("Trematode" 17).

Bester knew what readers wanted long before they knew what they wanted themselves. These days, most of us wouldn't bat an eye at the novel's depiction of sex, violence, and profanity. There are YA novels grittier than *Stars*. The novel's transgressions have evaporated into the cultural ether. So have its characters and landscapes. For starters, check out Hong Kong or Dubai; both cities currently surpass any urban space that Bester describes in terms of architecture alone. As for characters— look at, say, TikTok, where the most popular influencers exist as ridiculous cartoon versions of themselves. It's the inevitable "nature" of media technoculture, as McLuhan predicted at the same time Bester was working on his own inadvertent prophesies.

Granted, there were rules Bester couldn't break. He couldn't have his characters using expletives like *shit* or *fuck*, for example, and he could only describe sex acts via implication and innuendo. Had he written this novel in the twenty-first century, the gutter tongue—good in theory, goofy in practice—would probably sound and look nothing like it does when Gully speaks it. Nonetheless, *Stars* stands the test of time more than most SF novels. "Nothing dates harder and faster and more strangely than the future," Neil Gaiman reminds us, and yet *Stars* is "less dated than most cyberpunk" (vii, x). In some ways, it's less dated than *everything* that succeeded it and more imaginative than whatever is being passed off as SF today.

THESIS AND OUTLINE

My overarching thesis in this monograph is that *Stars* mapped new terrain in postwar SF and remains a polestar to this day. More specifically, the novel accomplishes what pre-1950s SF novels failed to do in terms of *style*, *structure*, and *attitude*. With *Stars*, Bester innovated and elevated these elements in a fell swoop, catapulted by the trebuchet of *The Demolished Man*.

In addition to this introduction, there are four chapters and a coda. Chapter one, "Literary Influences and Cyberpunk Previsions," explores Bester's hysterical inscription of literary tropes and allusions in the text; such excessiveness aligns *Stars* with a history of literature and points toward the future of SF while demonstrating an anxiety about authorial identity and complementing the various excesses that fuel the novel. In chapter two, "The Frankenstein Riff," I discuss the relationship between *Stars* and *Frankenstein*, both of which tell the stories of charismatic monsters and meta-referentially point to the inherent mad scientism of Shelley's and Bester's authorship as well as narrative itself. I focus on issues of class, gender, and race in the third chapter, "Architectures of Psyche, Power, and Patriarchy," examining how Bester, a product of his own patriarchal culture (and SF's endorsement of that culture), is at once progressive and regressive. "Speaking in Gutter Tongues" is the fourth and final chapter where I address the theme of religion in its assorted permutations with an eye to the religious subtext of Bester's linguistic flourishes and convolutions. The coda reaffirms that *Stars* signals the beginning of a new trend in SF, but the novel is also a tombstone looming over the genre's resting place in the graveyard of the twentieth century.

A NOTE ON SCHOLARSHIP

Compared to other prominent SF authors, scholarship on Bester's life and work is limited. There are no book-length biographies. Jad Smith includes ample biographical information, though, and many critics have recounted Bester's precarious relationship with SF. So has Bester himself. Published in 2016, Smith's outstanding monograph contains a chapter on *Stars* and discusses the novel in tandem with "Fondly Fahrenheit," which exhibits similar traits; it also addresses principal themes, narrative style, historical context, and critical reception. The chapter is an engaged overview, and for my purposes, Smith provides well-researched background material and ideas for greater elaboration and commentary. The other monograph published on Bester's oeuvre (also titled *Alfred Bester*) by Carolyn Wendell was released in 1982, six years before the author's death in 1987. It's a satisfactory primer, but it doesn't account for later works (e.g., *Golem^{100}* and *The Deceivers*), and it's far more limited in scope than Smith's study. Wendell's short chapter on *Stars* centers on gender relations and femininity. She has strong insights that inform my reading.

There are fewer than 10 formal scholarly articles on or related to *Stars* dating back to Jeff Riggenbach's "Science Fiction as Will and Idea: The World of Alfred Bester," published in 1972 in *Riverside Quarterly*. Perhaps the best article—and the one that got me interested in *Stars* as a graduate student—is Patrick A. McCarthy's "Science Fiction as Creative Revisionism: The Example of Alfred Bester's *The Stars My Destination*," which appeared in *Science Fiction Studies* in 1983. McCarthy's legwork scaffolds my first chapter and led to some of my central ideas. Beyond these essays and several others, I rely on reviews, interviews, and additional secondary sources from scholarly and popular venues. Bester's own essays about his craft, life, and career have been most interesting and helpful, but as a novelist myself, I'm acutely aware that what an author says about oneself is often not what an author actually *thinks*, let alone what the author *is*. For the literary critic, things become meaningful when they become repetitive, so I try to converge on what Bester said about his writing, SF, and relevant issues with consistency over the years.

References

Asimov, Isaac. "In Memoriam: Alfred Bester 1913–1987." *Nebula Awards 23*, edited by Michael Bishop. New York: Harcourt Brace Javanovich, 1987. 24–27.

Bester, Alfred. "A Diatribe Against Science Fiction." 1961. *Redemolished*. New York: iBooks, 2000. 431–35.

———. "Alfred Bester: The Stars and Other Destinations." Interview by James Phillips. *Starlog: The Science Fiction Universe* 128 (March 1988): 34–36, 72.

———. "Comment on 'Fondly Fahrenheit.'" *Starlight: The Great Short Fiction of Alfred Bester*. Garden City: Nelson Doubleday, 1976.

———. "My Affair with Science Fiction." 1975. *Redemolished*. New York: iBooks, 2000. 443–76.

———. "Science Fiction and the Renaissance Man." 1959. *Redemolished*. New York: iBooks, 2000. 408–30.

———. *The Demolished Man*. 1953. New York: Vintage, 1996.

———. "The Perfect Composite Science Fiction Author." 1961. *Redemolished*. New York: iBooks, 2000. 436–42.

———. *The Stars My Destination*. 1956. New York: Vintage, 1996.

———. "The Trematode: A Critique of Modern Science Fiction." *The Best Science Fiction Stories: 1953*, edited by Everett F. Bleiler and T.E. Dikty. New York: Frederick Fell, Inc., 1953. 11–22.

Bier, Jesse. "The Masterpiece in Science Fiction: Power or Parody?" *Journal of Popular Culture* 12.4 (Spring 1979): 604–10.

Bishop, Michael. Preface to "In Memoriam: Alfred Bester 1913–1987." *Nebula Awards 23*. New York: Harcourt Brace Jovanovich, 1989. 22–24.

Delany, Samuel R. "About Five Thousand, One Hundred and Seventy-Five Words." *SF: The Other Side of Realism*, edited by Thomas Clareson. Bowling Green: Bowling Green University Press, 1971. 130–46.

Flood, Leslie. "Book Reviews." *New Worlds* 50 (August 1956): 126–28.

Gaiman, Neil. "Of Time, and Gully Foyle." *The Stars My Destination*. New York: Vintage Books, 1996. vii–x.

Hipolito, Jane and Willis E. McNelly. "The Statement Is the Self: Alfred Bester's Science Fiction." *The Stellar Gauge: Essays on Science Fiction Writers*, edited by Michael J. Tolley and Kirpal Singh. Victoria: Norstrilia Press, 1980. 63–90.

Kelleghan, Fiona. "*The Stars My Destination* by Alfred Bester." *The Greenwood Encyclopedia of Science Fiction*. Westport: Greenwood Publishing, 2005. 1271–73.

Knight, Damon. *In Search of Wonder*. Chicago: Advent, 1967.

McLuhan, Marshall. *The Mechanical Bride: Folklore of Industrial Man*. 1951. In *Essential McLuhan*, edited by Eric McLuhan and Frank Zingrone. New York: Basic Books, 1995. 21–34.

———. *Understanding Media: The Extensions of Man*. 1962. Berkeley: Ginko Press, 2017.

Miller, P. Schuyler. Review of *The Stars My Destination*. *Astounding Science Fiction* 60.3 (November 1957): 148.

Nicholls, Peter. "Alfred Bester: New York, 2175 A.D." *The Washington Post*. May 25, 1980. https://www.washingtonpost.com/archive/entertainment/books/1980/05/25/alfred-bester-new-york-2175-ad/47b2bcc3-6679-45b5-93bc-59982349834f. Accessed October 26, 2020.

Platt, Charles. "Attack-Escape." *New Worlds Quarterly #4.* New York: Berkley Books, 1972. 210–20.

Raucci, Richard. "Introduction." *Redemolished.* New York: iBooks, 2000. 7–13.

Santesson, Stefan. "Universe in Books." *Fantastic Universe* 8.2 (August 1957): 111–13.

Smith, Jad. *Alfred Bester.* Chicago: University of Illinois Press, 2016.

Wendell, Carolyn. *Alfred Bester.* 1982. Cabin John: Wildside Press, 2006.

Williams, Paul. "Introduction." *The Stars My Destination.* Boston: Gregg Press, 1975. x–xv.

CHAPTER 2

Synopsis

Abstract Set in a pyrotechnic twenty-fifth century, Alfred Bester's *The Star's My Destination* is the story of Gully Foyle, a "stereotype Comman Man" who becomes a technologized Overman.

Keywords Sci-fi · Cyberpunk · Technology · Violence · Capitalism · Inner space

Part I

Prologue

In an overpopulated, war-torn twenty-fifth century, eleven trillion people inhabit three planets and eight moons. A scientific researcher, Charles Fort Jaunte, discovers teleportation in a laboratory on Callisto. How it works is a mystery, but every human being has the innate, neurological capacity to enact this evolutionary "Tigroid Function" and Cartesian phenomenon (i.e., "I think, therefore I jaunte"), which requires learned visualization, concentration, and blind faith. The practice spreads throughout the solar system, but only on planet surfaces; nobody has ever successfully jaunted across outer space. Regardless, the "Jaunte Age"

D. Harlan Wilson, *Alfred Bester's The Stars My Destination*, Palgrave Science Fiction and Fantasy: A New Canon, https://doi.org/10.1007/978-3-030-96946-2_2

effects widespread political, social, and economic upheaval, producing an interplanetary culture that is as spectacular and transcendent as it is corrupt, degraded, and grotesque.

Chapter 1

Low-grade mechanic Gully Foyle has been stranded on the damaged spaceship *Nomad* between Mars and Jupiter. After six months, a freighter named *Vorga*, owned by the industrial clan Presteign of Terra, approaches the wreckage. Gully believes *Vorga* will save him, but it passes him by, and he swears revenge. Fueled by monomania, he tries to repair *Nomad* and chart a course toward Jupiter in hopes of rescue.

Chapter 2

Nomad drifts near the Sargasso Asteroid, a receptacle for space debris collected by its inhabitants, the Scientific People, for two centuries. Tattooed with intricate, gender-specific Māori masks, the Scientific People practice an aboriginal, mystical form of pseudo-science and fetishize technology. They retrieve *Nomad* and clean up Gully, who fades in and out of consciousness. Their priestly leader, J♂seph, marries him off to a girl named M♀ira. Gully escapes and the Inner Planets navy rescues him. He is shocked when he looks in a mirror and sees that his face bears a Māori tattoo with the word N♂MAD across his brow.

Chapter 3

Jaunte instructor Robin Wednesbury is a one-way telepath who can send but not receive thoughts. She teaches students with head injuries how to regain their ability to jaunte, an upper-class privilege. In order to jaunte somewhere, travelers must first see the destination with their own eyes, and lower classes can't afford extensive transportation costs. Gully becomes Robin's student. She suspects him of being a malingerer with an ulterior motive. He admits to locating *Vorga*'s owner, Presteign of Presteign, a powerful Neo-Victorian clansman. Then he rapes her, threatening to turn her in if she gets in the way of his vengeance—according to postwar bylaws, Robin is a spy for Callisto hiding out on the Inner Planets. Elsewhere, Presteign hires Saul Dagenham, a professional courier and former physicist, to kidnap Gully and find a mysterious substance called PyrE. Presteign visits his daughter Olivia, a beautiful, blind albino. He retires to his Wall Street castle to swear in a new Mr. Presto, one of the hundreds of androids that manage his luxury department stores, and he jaunts to an inauguration ceremony for a new freighter in Vancouver. Gully infiltrates the ceremony. He attempts to blow up *Vorga*, but an anti-gravity beam deflects the dirty bomb he hurls at the ship. Presteign orders his minions to apprehend him.

Chapter 4

In Castle Presteign's Star Chamber, Central Intelligence Captain Peter Y'ang-Yeovil informs Presteign and his lawyer Regis Sheffield that *Nomad* had been transporting the world's supply of PyrE, a powerful warhead. Central Intelligence wants it. Y'ang-Yeovil bargains for Gully, thinking he knows the location of *Nomad*, but when Presteign's ally Saul Dagenham arrives, the outnumbered Y'ang-Yeovil departs in consternation. A fission-blast accident has turned Dagenham into a radioactive "Typhoid Mary"; he must avoid prolonged physical contact with other people. A specialist in theft and espionage, Dagenham was hired by Presteign to extract information about *Nomad* from Gully, who has been confined to an isolation tank in a Mexico City psychiatric hospital. So far, Gully hasn't caved. Dagenham returns to the hospital and subjects Gully to two methods of psycho-surreal torture: Nightmare Theater and Megal Mood. Neither method works; Gully's resolve is ironclad.

Chapter 5

Incarcerated in the abysmal French sanitarium Gouffre Martel, Gully sinks into depression, psychosis, catatonia. Jaunting free is impossible as the coordinates to the sanitarium are unknown to prisoners. The only means of escape is a suicidal "Blue Jaunte" into nothingness. Gully befriends fellow prisoner Jisbella "Jiz" McQueen. She gives him elocution lessons. Dagenham visits and notices that Gully no longer speaks exclusively in the gutter tongue, a hallmark of his lower-class upbringing. Dagenham never told Gully about PyrE; he only said that *Nomad* had been carrying precious bullion. He offers Gully ten percent of the payload to lead him to *Nomad*. Gully agrees on the condition of his parole. Dagenham suspects he's in cahoots with Y'ang-Yeovil and rescinds the offer. Gully knocks him cold, then he and Jiz escape from Gouffre Martel through a vast underground gorge. They emerge onto a grassy plain at night where they make love and await the morning.

Chapter 6

At a Freak Factory in New Jersey, Dr. Harley Baker surgically removes the tattoo from Gully's face. Gully makes a deal with Jiz's old partner-in-crime Sam Quatt to use his pleasure yacht, the Saturn Weekender, so he can return to *Nomad* and uncover the real payload. He knows the bullion is a subterfuge for something else. Gully doesn't mention the bullion to Jiz, and she thinks he wants it all for himself. Dagenham organizes a raid on the Freak Factory, killing Quatt. Gully and Jiz jaunte to Long Island where the Weekender is quartered. At Courier Headquarters, Dagenham reveals to Sheffield that he orchestrated everything Gully has done, including his escape from Gouffre Martel. Gully's ingenuity surprised him, and he demonstrated a singular force of will. Dagenham resolves to shadow Gully and follow him to *Nomad*.

Chapter 7

On the Weekender, Jiz removes the bandages from Gully's face. The surgery appears to be a success. They land on the Sargasso Asteroid and encounter J♂seph. Gully's face flushes with anger and his tattoo becomes visible, red now instead of black; deeply embedded scar tissue brings out the color. The tattoo had been the only way his enemies could identify him—they don't know what Gully looks like beneath it. Now he has to subdue his emotions in order to subvert his enemies and remain incognito. The Scientific People have embedded *Nomad* in the asteroid. Gully fights them off as he searches the ship. He and Jiz uncover a safe, but it's too heavy. They wire it with explosives. Gully returns to the Weekender, takes off. Jiz ignites the explosives and Gully collects the safe as it flies into the atmosphere. Jiz jetpacks after him, but Dagenham and his crew show up. Gully abandons Jiz and blasts away.

Part II

Chapter 8

Amid the first Solar Wars, Gully adopts the identity of superrich entertainer Geoffrey Fourmyle of Ceres, ringleader of the Four Mile Circus. In Green Bay, Wisconsin, he presides over festivities like a slapstick Shakespearean clown, clever and calculating yet outlandish, asinine, and vulgar. His entire body has been enhanced with illicit implants that transform him into a formidable cyborg, more machinic than human. He jauntes to Robin Wednesbury's apartment complex, which has been gutted and looted by homeless "Jack-jaunters." Gully deflects the Jacks that attack him, accelerating into fasttime mode. Robin isn't there; she has been confined to a local hospital after trying to commit suicide. He abducts her from the hospital. At first, Robin doesn't know that the famous superfool is actually Gully. He wants to exploit her one-way telepathic powers and use her as a ventriloquist to help him navigate upper-class society. Gully becomes anxious when he thinks he hears a Blue Jaunte; his tattoo flares, exposing his true identity. The Four Mile Circus is a front for his revenge plot, he explains, and *Vorga* may have been transporting refugees off of Callisto, including Robin's mother and sisters. Confronted with Hobson's choice, Robin agrees to help, but she vows payback to Gully for raping and blackmailing her.

Chapter 9

Gully makes his debut with Robin on New Year's Eve at a government ball in Canberra, the capital of Australia, where he tracked *Vorga* crewman Ben Forrest, one of three leads to whoever gave the order to leave him for dead. The other two leads are Angelo Poggi, an Italian cook, and Sergei Orel, a Russian quack doctor. With Robin in his mind's ear, Gully dispels rumors about Geoffrey Fourmyle's bad behavior to high-society socialites, passing himself off as a refined, charming tycoon with a backstory that foregrounds his business exploits. The mayor of the Aussie Cannery company town gives them a tour. They come across a gathering of "Cellar Christians." Organized religion is illegal, so these apostates must worship in private speakeasies. Forrest is among them, high on a psychoactive drug called Analogue. Gully crashes the service and captures Forrest, who drowns during interrogation, giving up nothing. As if in response to this act of savagery, a fiery apparition materializes—a "Burning Man" who looks exactly like Gully.

Chapter 10

In Shanghai, China, Gully and Robin attend a costume party and visit the office of Dr. Orel, pretending to be new patients. A built-in suicide implant kills Orel before he can convey any incriminating intel. The Burning Man reappears and sets the office on fire. Gully and Robin jaunte to the Spanish Stairs in Rome, looking for Angelo Poggi. He died long ago, but Y'ang-Yeovil has assumed his identity, staking out the Stairs with his commandos and reconfiguring his body in the image of the former *Vorga* cook. Y'ang-Yeovil belies his cover with an offbeat speech pattern as Gully asks him questions. A fight breaks out and the Burning Man reappears again, distracting the commandos. Gully and Robin jaunte away.

Chapter 11

Presteign hosts a New Year's Eve celebration at his Central Park mansion. Undercover as Fourmyle of Ceres, Gully arrives with Robin in a flourish of pomp and circumstance. Presteign introduces him to his daughter Olivia, who captivates him, then Dagenham, who doesn't recognize him. As usual, Robin provides Gully with telepathic guidance. He sees Jiz at the party. Now she's a courier for Dagenham as well as his lover. Gully learns that PyrE, not bullion, was the real payload on *Nomad*. He retrieved the PyrE from the safe, but he doesn't know what it is. Jiz refuses to tell him as payback for abandoning her on the Sargasso Asteroid. Suddenly, the Outer Satellites bomb Terra. Gully and Olivia watch the bombardment from a rooftop garden. On the war-ravaged New York streets, Gully kills a group of Jacks that attack him and reconnoiters with Robin at the Four Mile Circus in Old St. Patrick's Cathedral. In a letter on Orel's desk, she found a new lead, Rodger Kempsey, another *Vorga* crewman who now resides on the moon. Gully needs her to coach him one last time. When he concedes to falling in love with Olivia, though, Robin promises to destroy him and jaunte away.

Chapter 12

At Central Intelligence headquarters in London, Y'ang-Yeovil appraises the damage from the Outer Satellites' New Year's Eve bombing. Determined to save her mother and sisters, Robin rats out Gully. In New York, Olivia informs Presteign that she saw a pattern on Fourmyle of Ceres's face—the pattern of a devil mask that blows his cover. Meanwhile, Jiz tells Dagenham who Geoffrey Fourmyle really is, confirming his suspicions, and Gully captures Kempsey at Mare Nubium, an ecological outpost on the moon. He surgically removes Kempsey's heart but keeps him alive. Kempsey says *Vorga* had been transporting 600 refugees from Callisto. Rather than usher the refugees to their destination, the crew robbed and murdered them at the behest of Captain Lindsey Joyce. A Martian Skoptsy, Joyce gave the order to bypass *Nomad*. Gully sees the Burning Man and thinks it's a guardian angel. He worries that he won't be able to sufficiently punish Joyce because Skoptsys lack sensory perception and the ability to experience pain and pleasure. He sets a course to Mars. Kempsey dies during takeoff, and for the first time, Gully feels remorse for his vengeful actions.

Chapter 13

Presteign, Dagenham, and Y'ang-Yeovil all dispatch warrants for Geoffrey Fourmyle a.k.a. Gully Foyle, "Solar Enemy Number One." On Mars, Gully kidnaps Sigurd Magsman, the planet's only fully functional telepath, to help him track down Captain Joyce. This ancient child takes him to a monastery in the Skoptsy Colony. In addition to being sensory deprived, Skoptsys are eunuchs who believe sex is evil and live like ascetic monks. Gully follows Magsman's telepathic lead into a catacomb where the slug-like Skoptsys exist in a somnambulistic haze. Joyce turns out to be a woman, bewildering Gully. In the Jaunte Age, women must practice purdah for their own "protection," and Joyce had to masquerade as a man, working her way to officer rank in the merchant marine. The Burning Man returns and speaks for the first time, divulging that the order to forsake *Vorga* originated with Olivia. Commandos swarm the monastery. As they close in, the Outer Satellites attack Mars. Gully jauntes to his ship and loses consciousness during takeoff due to gravitational pressure.

Chapter 14

Gully awakens strapped to a bed on *Vorga* orbiting Terra. Olivia saved him. He confesses his love for her. She confesses that she betrayed him to her father, but she says she loves him, too. She hates being a blind freak and wants other people to suffer like her. She and Gully have common ground in misanthropy and vengeance. Olivia wants him to turn over the PyrE to Presteign. Her father will use it to commit genocide, but she doesn't care as long as they can be together. In a moment of enlightenment, Gully grows a conscience and realizes he has changed, matured, wizened—the tiger in him has died. He wants to set things right. Dagenham, Y'ang-Yeovil, Presteign, and Jiz assemble in the Star Chamber. If they can't recover the PyrE, the Outer Satellites will defeat the Inner Planets and destroy them. They must overcome their differences and work together to capture Gully. When they hear that the prodigal daughter has absconded with him, Presteign has an epileptic seizure, then reveals that PyrE is made of the same primordial protomatter that generated the Universe. Furthermore, like jaunting, PyrE requires psychokinetic activation and can only be released by "Will and Idea." They devise a plan to blow up the Four Mile Circus with trace amounts of PyrE, using Robin's one-way telepathic powers to subatomically trigger it. In Russia, Gully consults Sheffield to defend him for a slew of crimes including robbery, rape, blackmail, murder, treason, and genocide. Outfitted with cybernetic enhancements, he overpowers Gully, drugs him, and jauntes to Old St. Patrick's Cathedral where the Four Mile Circus has been ransacked by Jacks. Sheffield is really an Outer Satellite spy. He recounts how a raider incapacitated *Nomad*, picked up a half-dead Gully, and deposited him in space 600,000 miles sunward. The idea was to lure in and destroy Inner Satellite ships responding to his distress signals, but true to his surname, Gully *foiled* their plans by accomplishing a space-jaunte back to *Nomad*. As nobody has ever space-jaunted before, the Outer Satellites are just as interested in acquiring PyrE as Gully so that they can decipher how he pulled off the feat. In Central Intelligence's New York office, Sheffield's assistant Bunny brings Y'ang-Yeovil up to speed, but it's too late: Robin psychokinetically ignites the PyrE.

Chapter 15

Previously, Gully sent out slugs of PyrE for examination by scientists to figure out its properties and capabilities. Prompted by Robin's thought waves, the slightest particle of PyrE residua erupts into earth-shaking fire-bombs. A tenth of a gram reduces Old St. Pat's to rubble. Presteign, Dagenham, Y'ang-Yeovil, Robin, Jiz, and a team of operatives and commandos flock to the ruins. They uncover Sheffield's corpse. Gully fell through the floor, but he's still alive, trapped in a crevasse with clothes and tattoo ablaze. In an effort to escape, he experiences a fit of synesthesia and jaunts forward and backward in time, rendering him the Burning Man. In the future, Robin telepathically guides him back to Old St. Pat's.

Chapter 16

In the Star Chamber, Presteign and Dagenham press Gully to give up the PyrE. Jiz, on the other hand, wants him to destroy it, whereas Y'ang-Yeovil wants to know how he space-jaunted. Gully demands to be punished, purged, freed from the weight of his conscience. He used to be a robot, driven by the one-track mind of vengeance. Now he recognizes that he is a more complicated being, a "freak of the universe" who must hone his skills and teach everybody else how to be the best they can be. Followed by his captors, Gully jaunts to prominent world stages and distributes PyrE slugs to the people, moralizing about class divisions and social responsibility, challenging humanity to band together, to put an end to war, to reach for the titular stars. Inspired by this newfound "faith in faith," he jaunts through space and time to the outermost expanses of the universe, then returns to *Nomad*. Several years have passed since his initial encounter with the Scientific People. M♀ira and J♂seph find him asleep in a tool locker curled into a fetal ball. Acknowledging his penance and divinity, they prepare for his awakening and symbolic rebirth.

CHAPTER 3

Cyberpunk Previsions and Literary Influences

Abstract Bester's imagined futures drew heavily from the history of literature and mapped lines of flight for the SF genre. In *Stars*, he establishes himself as a son of the pulp-SF and high-modernist writers that preceded him and a forefather to the New Wave and cyberpunk movements that followed his lead. Bester enacts wordplay and carefully devised the names of characters and places. These tactics situate *Stars* within a literary tradition that deepens the significance of the novel. So does the novel's rampant intertextuality, which points toward the future of SF while demonstrating an anxiety about authorial identity and complementing the various excesses that fuel Bester's pyrotechnic impetus. Awakening is a dominant, correlating theme. It allows Bester to map Gully's transformation from sleeper to seer and make further commentary on the shortcomings of SF.

Keywords Cyberpunk · Literary · Modernism · Intertextuality · Awakening

© The Author(s), under exclusive license to Springer Nature
Switzerland AG 2022
D. Harlan Wilson, *Alfred Bester's The Stars My Destination*,
Palgrave Science Fiction and Fantasy: A New Canon,
https://doi.org/10.1007/978-3-030-96946-2_3

BESTER'S WASTEBASKET

Bester's imagined futures drew heavily from the history of literature and mapped lines of flight for the SF genre. In *Stars*, he establishes himself as a son of the pulp-SF and high-modernist writers that preceded him and a forefather to the New Wave and cyberpunk movements that chased his dragon.

So many movements are reactionary and induced by undesirable status quos. Propelled by Michael Moorcock and his editorship of *New Worlds*, the New Wave took its cue from experimental French cinema, reacting to the premium that genre SF placed on hard technologies and scientific application. New Wave icons like Brian Aldiss and J.G. Ballard deemphasized science, technology, and so-called reality in favor of psychology, cognition, and surreality. The concept of inner space is probably the best indicator of New Wave aesthetics. As Ballard famously stated: "The biggest developments of the immediate future will take place, not on the Moon or Mars, but on Earth, and it is *inner* space, not outer, that needs to be explored. The only truly alien planet is Earth. In the past the scientific bias of s-f has been towards the physical sciences—rocketry, electronics, cybernetics—and the emphasis should switch to the biological sciences" (197).

New Wave authors adopted the experimental techniques of high modernism, a twentieth-century interwar movement that was a reaction to popular culture and the dumbing down of art and literature. High modernists like James Joyce, Gertrude Stein, Ezra Pound, and Virginia Woolf all disrupted conventional narration in favor of more dynamic, complex modes of expression that accounted for new cultural formations and fallout, among them the horrors of modern warfare, technological advancement, and the advent of cinema and psychoanalysis. Cyberpunk also reacted to old trends in SF, but it was really a New Wave extension—the postmodern version of its modernist precursor. Whereas the New Wave took its cue from a variety of cultural developments, however, cyberpunk was preoccupied with the pathological aggression of late capitalist image-culture. Hence Frederic Jameson's thesis that it was the "supreme literary expression if not of postmodernism, then of late capitalism itself" (419).

Stars's detractor P. Schuyler Miller was actually the first person to use the term "New Wave" in reference to the movement that put Bester on a pedestal. This was in 1961 in his column "The Reference Library" for

Analog (Nicholls, "New"). Miller cites Brian Aldiss and John Brunner as figureheads, but the New Wave didn't really take shape until Moorcock's ascension.

As Jad Smith recounts, Bester's

> reputation grew exponentially due to the rising influence of the New Wave. When [...] Moorcock took the helm of *New Worlds* in 1964 and determined to set the magazine—and SF in general—on a bold new course, he championed Bester's work, representing it as one of the few bridges between the Golden Age and the new future he and other New Wave writers imagined for SF. From 1963 forward, Moorcock would cite *The Stars My Destination* in particular as an example of "grown up" science fiction that could be held to the highest literary standard and withstand all but the "most rigorous criticism." (168)

Cyberpunks loved Bester for the same reason. His attention to style and psyche has clear linkages with the novels and stories of authors like William Gibson, Bruce Sterling, Rudy Rucker, John Shirley, and Pat Cadigan. Gibson even referred to *Stars* as a guiding light and "talisman" for *Neuromancer*, cyberpunk's definitive novel ("*Stars*"). "In many respects his work was a forerunner of cyberpunk. He is one of the very few genre-sf writers to have bridged the chasm between the old [guard] and the New Wave, by becoming a legendary figure for both—perhaps because in his sf imagery he conjured up, with bravura, both outer and inner space" (Nicholls, "Bester").

This isn't to say that Bester knew or cared much about the New Wave or cyberpunk despite being around long enough to see the latter movement reach its apex. When he returned to the SF genre in the 1970s during the third act of his career, New Wave affiliates revered him. True to his nature, Bester made no pretensions. "I know almost nothing about New Wave science fiction," he wrote in a letter to Anthony Boucher and J. Francis McComas. "All I can say is that I welcome anything new, am always most sympathetic to the breaking away from old traditions which have a tendency to fossilize" (qtd. in Smith 168). This is the credo that Bester's best work lives by. Embracing the spirit of Pound's sacred plea to "Make It New," he exacted a go-for-broke intensity and consistently tried to reinvent himself, dissatisfied with established forms and hateful toward narrative sameness, regurgitation, and banality.

With the exception of less censorship, the state of the publishing industry in the twenty-first century is not that different from Bester's heyday. Editors and publishers of the speculative genres are limited in scope, although they don't think they are. They think they know what originality is, but almost invariably, the New, in their eyes, turns out to be the same old sheep in another sheep's clothing. Big SF publishers like Tor and smaller presses like Apex Book Company would both bounce something like *Golem*[100] with extreme prejudice for not complying with the prescription of what they deem to be innovative. The same goes for contemporary, award-winning SF magazines such as *Lightspeed* and *Clarkesworld*, whose editors say they want "original" stories when in fact they want predictable characters and categorical storylines that abide by a strict rubric. In short, SF must obey their rules—otherwise it's no good.

Moreover, older periodicals like *The Magazine of Fantasy & Science Fiction* and *Interzone* seem to have taken a step backward; they were more progressive in the 1980s. This makes sense. People now watch and listen to images more than they read words. We have forgotten how to read. *Moby-Dick* (1851), for instance, might as well have been written by an alien from another dimension: the depth of Melville's allusions alone is entirely lost on twenty-first-century generations. In order to cater to the largest readership possible, magazines and publishers require writing that accounts for this collective loss. But SF should have never regarded itself as *the* genre of innovation—not then, and certainly not now, as the wind-blown ashes of the genre drift from screen to screen. Bester would have been appalled by today's SF. He probably would have been relegated to obscure indie presses, the last outpost for genuine imaginative literature. James Joyce's *Ulysses* (1922) had trouble getting published 100 years ago. It's totally unpublishable today. If nobody knew who Joyce was, even a small press wouldn't touch it. Too long; too complex. Above all: too artistic, creative, and intelligent.

Of course, Bester loved Joyce. He idolized *Ulysses* as a young writer, and *Portrait of the Artist as a Young Man* (1916) is a key intertext in *Stars*. Joyce's experimental, visionary prose and subject matter served as a beacon for almost every subsequent literary writer that aimed for the New. Given their focus on technology, inner space, and linguistic mad scientism, I would argue that *Ulysses* and *Finnegans Wake* (1939) are two of the twentieth century's most important SF novels, even if they are generally categorized as literary and/or fantastic fiction. They certainly fed the imaginations of New Wave and cyberpunk authors, but few novels so effectively integrate and build upon Joycean rubrics like *Stars*. In broader terms, Bester was so inventive that he made it difficult for anybody else to outdo him. As K.W. Jeter once said: "What's being labeled as cyberpunk is just the usual rediscovery of Alfred Bester that happens every two or three years in the SF field. Almost everything labeled as cyberpunk, just as with almost any supposedly new thing in SF, really resembles nothing so much as Alfred Bester's closet. Or his wastebasket" (qtd. in Bishop 23–24).

Name Games and Adaptations

J.G. Ballard's most experimental work, *The Atrocity Exhibition* (1970), exemplifies the New Wave in terms of style, substance, and attitude. This collection of "condensed novels" includes a chapter called "The Generations of America" that simply lists the names of real and fictional people who shoot one another. The first sentence sets the scene: "These are the generations of America" (159). Then the shooting begins: "Sirhan Sirhan shot Robert F. Kennedy. And Ethel M. Kennedy shot Judith Birnbaum. And Judith Birnbaum shot Elizabeth Bochnak. And Elizabeth Bochnak shot Andrew Witwer" (159). On and on he goes for five pages, concluding with this sentence: "And William Forbis shot Ingrid Carroll" (165).

"The Generations of America" is a playful, satirical thought-experiment about media pathology and violence in the 1960s. We recognize historical figures like Sirhan Sirhan and Robert F. Kennedy, but they're really just MacGuffins that propel the "plot." Ballard mainly uses obscure names. He lifted them from the mastheads of *Look*, *Life*, and *Time*, American magazines that he read dutifully and "helped to create the media landscape at the heart of *The Atrocity Exhibition*" (nt. 163). Fifteen years earlier, Bester did something similar, using English telephone directories and locales for character surnames in *Stars*. He was meticulous about which names he chose, as they would contribute to the melody of his prose. "It's hard work, but names are very important," he told James Phillips in a posthumously published interview for *Starlog*.

> I essentially write from a musical standpoint in terms of composition. First there's rhythm: a three-syllable name, a four, two, or one. They all have to be balanced against each other. I cannot write a story in which everyone has a one-syllable name. Then, having determined the syllable count, I

start to read the telephone directories, and all sort of name registries. I even have a copy of the social register. I read them constantly, and it sometimes takes me days to finally get the names, and the name must somehow be expressive of the character—not directly but just have a little of the character's color in terms of the name's sound and rhythm. ("Alfred" 36)

Gully Foyle, Olivia Presteign, Saul Dagenham, Robin Wednesbury, Jiz McQueen, Peter Y'ang-Yeovil, Regis Sheffield—most of the characters in *Stars* get their surnames from mass media within Bester's reach when he was drafting the novel in England. W&G Foyle Ltd., for instance, is an English bookstore chain founded in 1903, whereas Dagenham, Sheffield, and Yeovil are suburbs in London, Yorkshire, and Somerset. The derivation of these surnames from media reflects the novel's hyper-mediatized society, which, among other things, problematizes identity by linking it to commodity fetishism. Consider the "society notables" with whom Olivia fraternizes. "There was a Sears-Roebuck, a Gillette, young Sidney Kodak who would one day be Kodak of Kodak, a Houbigant, Buick of Buick, and R.H. Macy XVI, head of the powerful Saks-Gimbel clan" (*Stars* 45). These monikers foreshadow the terminal identity crisis of Max Barry's postcapitalist novel *Jennifer Government* (2003), where everybody assumes corporate surnames (even children) as a sign of commercial alliance, (cult) class status, and political economy. In both cases, surnames symptomatize an intrinsic cultural pathology that gestures toward Marshall McLuhan's idea of "the technological simulation of consciousness, when the creative process of knowing will be collectively and corporately extended to the whole of human society, much as we have already extended our senses and our nerves by the various media" (5).

Bester doesn't just select names for their acoustic and lyrical resonance. Many of them exude a keen multivalence. Gully Foyle is the crown jewel. Sharing his surname with a bookstore speaks to his evolution from ignorance and malevolence to knowledge and benevolence. The more one reads, the wiser one becomes, and by the end of the novel, Gully has become well-read not only in the workings of society, but in the flows of his desires with respect to society. The surname is a complex pun on the term *foil*, too, heralding his violence and aggression (as a fencing weapon), literary function (as a character whose contradistinction accentuates the traits of other characters), and capacity to frustrate and thwart the plans of his enemies (foiled again!). *Foil* also refers to the scent of a hunted animal, what Gully is to Presteign, Dagenham, and Y'ang-Yeovil. Furthermore, in *The Oxford English Dictionary*, an antiquated usage denotes "what is trampled underfoot; hence, manure, dung" ("Foil"). This is precisely how our anti-heroic prole is made to feel about himself by his twenty-fifth-century contemporaries and especially *Vorga*: when the freighter passes him by in the first chapter, it triggers his insecurities and lights the wildfire of his vengeance. Put simply, Gully feels badly because everybody looks down on him and treats him badly. His surname is the badge of his obloquy.

Likewise is Gully's first name a multivalent pun. The overt allusion to Jonathan Swift's *Gulliver's Travels* (1726) has been thoroughly documented. In an introduction to the 1975 reprint of *Stars*, Paul Williams says that Gully's "early adventures clearly parallel those of an earlier Gulliver: he is shipwrecked, and makes his way to an island—asteroid— floating in the sky, inhabited by fools who have made a religion of science. Bester's Sargasso Asteroid, inhabited by the self-named Scientific People, is easily as comic as Jonathan Swift's Laputa" (xii).

Gully and Gulliver are both lenses through which readers witness the spectacles of their fantastical worlds, and they both undergo a process of education and enlightenment. Contrary to Swift's novel, *Stars* concludes on a positive note. Wendell makes this insightful deduction, synching the connotation of the forename with the surname: "Unlike the original Gulliver, who spends his last days in a stable because he cannot bear his fellow human beings, Gully places his last bet on the Yahoos. He has awakened to a mystical fate—a possible savior of the world. In this process, he has become his own foil: the brutish, selfish lout has become the intelligent and active moral leader" (35). Patrick A. McCarthy identifies another ramification of the full name wherein Gully/Gulliver and Foyle/Foil form a bipolarity: "[A]s Gulliver he is akin to Swift's common man who undergoes uncommon adventures—a further possible allusion being to Gully Jimson, the Blakean artist of Joyce Cary's *The Horse's Mouth* (1944)—while 'Foyle' contains several potential meanings, among them an echo of Hopkins' declaration that 'the grandeur of God' will flame out [of the dull world], like shining from shook foil'" (59).

Unplugged from literary intertextuality, the name Gully signifies the gully or abyss that he must climb out of. This happens literally when he and Jiz escape from the French prison Gouffre Martel through an underground gorge. Metaphorically, Gully spends the novel escaping from the gorge of his own psyche and social (mal)construction.

Some readers didn't care for complexity of this nature. As I mentioned in my introduction, Jesse Bier associates *Star*'s "punningly derivative names" with Bester's pyrotechnic excess, which annoys him and breaks the Fourth Wall (605). Bier thinks Bester is just showing off. Jeff Riggenbach, on the other hand, takes the opposite stance, claiming that the "names Bester gives to his characters are often important clues to the relationship each character has to others. [For example], the Scientific People, who take Foyle from the *Nomad*, tattoo their faces to resemble Maori masks. They scientifically mate Foyle to a girl called M♀ira, an anagram for Maori" (174). Like them or not, Bester's name games situate *Stars* within a literary tradition that deepens the significance of the text.

Another name game related to *Stars* and some of Bester's other works concerns titles. Throughout his career, editors and publishers sporadically retitled his short and long fiction. It began with his contest-winning first story, "The Broken Axiom," which appeared in the April 1939 issue of *Thrilling Wonder Stories* and was originally called "Diaz-X." Looking back, Bester said that "Diaz-X" was "a ridiculous title" wisely replaced by the editors ("My Affair" 447). Other stories experienced similar renamings, as did three novels, usually in the interest of greater marketability. Bester's second, mainstream novel was published as *Who He?* (1953) by The Dial Press. Three years later, Berkley Books bought the rights and reprinted it as *The Rat Race* (1956). This is a more descriptive title with a familiar theme that expunges the mystery of *Who He?*, and yet it's quite redundant: Fantasy Publishing Company put out an SF novel called *The Rat Race* by Jay Franklin in 1950. Bester's fourth novel was serialized in *Analog* as *The Indian Giver* (1974–75), then published in the US by Berkeley as *The Computer Connection* (1975) and in the UK by Methuen as *Extro* (1975). In the 1970s, these changes probably had nothing to do with political correctness. Rather, the publishers wanted to capitalize on the novel's techno-SF appeal, siphoning Bester's genre renown and the buzz generated by *Demolished* and *Stars* two decades earlier.

None of Bester's books and stories wore more titular masks than *Stars*. Working titles included *Hell's My Destination*, *The Burning Spear*, *The Burning Man*, *Wide World's End*, and *Forest of the Night*. Bester decided on *Tyger! Tyger!*, using the archaic spelling to signal William Blake's inspirational poem, but the "y"s were replaced with the modernized "i"s by the UK publisher. *Tiger! Tiger!* captures the essence of the novel and its protagonist, but it doesn't invoke or even hint at anything science fictional. US editor Mac Tully wanted to siphon history, too, milking

Demolished's fame. Bester recounts: "Tully, who was then with NAL [New American Library], one of my publishers, did not want *Tyger! Tyger!* He said, 'We must have a science-fiction title.' I said, 'You're publishing it, you go ahead and title it" ("Alfred" 36).

Overall, the titles neither inhibited nor facilitated the novel's success. They rarely do. The content is the culprit. I like *Tyger! Tyger!* much more than *The Stars My Destination* in spite of the latter's inherent evocation. The keywords "Stars" and "Destination" suggest a space opera with inter-galactic travel, and the assertion "The Stars My Destination" is enigmatic by exclusion of a verb between "Stars" and "My" (e.g., "are," "were," "will be," etc.). Unfamiliar with Bester, I remember being intrigued when a professor assigned *Stars* to me in graduate school. Not until the end did I discover that the title came from a revised version of the nursery jingle that appears in the first chapter: "*Gully Foyle is my name / And Terra is my nation. / Deep space is my dwelling place / And death's my destination*" (16). An unevolved Gully recollects this jingle in the first chapter as he waits to die in *Nomad*. In the final chapter, the last line of the jingle becomes Mac Tully's US title, reflecting Gully's development and cosmic potential instead of his demise. It's a good title. It works as a lure and an earmark in itself as well as in relation to the text. But I'm not alone in thinking *Tiger! Tiger!* is more effective and representative of *Star*'s essence. William Gibson likes it better, observing that the Blakean label was "evidently deemed too arthouse for the trade." Sharing this sentiment, Neil Gaiman underscores its literary import:

> When I read this book […] in the 1970s, as a young teenager, I read it under the title *Tiger! Tiger!* It's a title I prefer to the rather more upbeat *The Stars My Destination*. It is a title of warning, of admiration. God, we are reminded in Blake's poem, created the tiger too. The God who made the lamb also made the carnivores that prey upon it. And Gully Foyle, our hero, is a predator. We meet him and are informed that he is everyman, a nonentity; then Bester lights the touch paper, and we stand back and watch him flare and burn and illuminate: almost literate, stupid, single-minded, amoral (not in the hip sense of being too cool for morality, but simply utterly, blindly selfish), he is a murdered—perhaps a multiple murderer—a rapist, a monster. A tiger. (ix)

Coincidentally, *Star*'s titular vicissitudes reflect its textual vicissitudes. Between its serialization in *Galaxy*, UK and US runs, and later reprints, there are several versions of the manuscript. Gary K. Wolfe explains that the texts of the first three printings "vary significantly, and Bester's original typescript, along with correspondence and other documents associated with the novel's early publication history, is not known to have survived. A comparison of the three texts suggests that each was prepared separately—probably from carbon copies of the typescript—and each varies uniquely at many points" (814). For this study, I use the 1996 Vintage Books edition, which is endorsed by the Estate of Alfred Bester and combines material from earlier versions. The copyright page gives credit to Byron Preiss Visual Publications (BPVP), a subsidiary but not unrelated outfit.

Byron Preiss was an American author, editor, and book packager "influenced by the Bauhaus school, whose graphic designers tested the limits of tradition" (Preiss 5). In the 1970s, BPVP spurred the rise of graphic novels and the initiative to establish comics as a reputable artistic medium. Between 1976 and 1979, BPVP produced nine graphic novels, including a two-volume adaptation of *Stars* illustrated by Howard Chaykin and typeset by Alex Jay. Preiss met with considerable resistance from just about everybody in the industry, "attacked by fans and comic professionals for betraying the very medium he professed to uplift" (Williams, "Strange" 102). I don't know what kind of relationship Bester had with Preiss; there is little documentation. In light of their mutual pursuit of originality for mature, erudite readers, I suspect they would have had something to talk about.

BPVP's *Stars* is an impressive, pioneering accomplishment whose painted, Rockwellesque artwork and rhizomatic panel arrangement augments Bester's own style and acumen. Putting it together wasn't easy, and like Bester's *Stars*, the comic exists in different formats. According to Preiss, Bester, "the Orson Welles of science fiction," gave him and Chaykin "carte blanche to do what we wanted with *Stars* as long as the original was respected" (5). Published by Baronet Books in 1979, volume one covers the prologue and first part of Bester's two-part novel. It sold relatively well. Shortly thereafter, Baronet went under, and an excerpt from the unfinished second installment appeared the same year in the comics magazine *Heavy Metal*. Also released was a signed limited edition of volume one in a slipcase with space for volume two, but it would be over a decade before the complete graphic novel saw the light of day.

Preiss and Chaykin's adaptation stands as "one of the first sophisticated 'full color' American graphic novels" (ibid.). In addition, it is the most sophisticated rendition of *Stars* in other media. A feature film has been in development for decades. Many writers, directors, and producers have flirted with an adaptation, but nobody has been able to bring Bester's vision to bear.

Kong: Skull Island (2017) director Jordan Vogt-Roberts is the most recent filmmaker associated with *Stars*. In a 2017 interview, he rued the undertaking, calling himself a masochist with a "stupid knack for wanting to take on projects that people call unfilmable." This isn't to say that he doesn't love the book. Nor is he unfamiliar with its reputation and influence. "A lot of sci-fi from that era, when you read it, it was incredible ideas, just some of the most thoughtful things you've encountered," said Vogt-Roberts, "but it was ultimately very dry. [Bester's work is] so explosive. It's literally like each page of *The Stars My Destination* almost has enough ideas in it that could fill an entire movie normally. *Stars* is borderline one of those books like *Neuromancer* or *John Carter* [...] that has almost been deeply mined for its ideas already, except I still think there's an incredible amount of relevance to it and I think that the ending of that book sticks the landing in such a profound way."

Since that interview, it appears Vogt-Roberts has respected his masochistic tendency and opted out of the project. On IMDb.com, there are no directors or production companies associated with the adaptation at the time of this writing. The state of contemporary FX could certainly render a compelling spectacle and account for Bester's various extrapolations. The *X-Men* franchise's Nightcrawler, for example, is a bona fide jaunter whose ability to teleport has been depicted onscreen with remarkable verisimilitude, dating back to his first appearance in *X2: X-Men United* (2003), and in *X-Men: Apocalypse* (2016), Quicksilver shows us what Gully might look like when he accelerates his cyborg body and slips into fasttime. Vogt-Roberts rightly asserts that *Stars* oozes ideas from every pore, but it's nothing like the stream-of-consciousness density of *Finnegans Wake* or *Ulysses*. It may have been unfilmable in the twentieth century. Not in the twenty-first century. I can easily envision a six-episode limited series that does justice to the novel. Bester's prose has always been cinematic. Cinema has finally caught up to it.

Stars has bled into other media, with writers using Bester's name and namings as Easter eggs. "Jaunting" is the method of teleportation in the British TV series *The Tomorrow People* (1973–79), and Stephen King's story "The Jaunt" (1981) takes its name from the novel's central artifice. Alfred Bester is a character on the 1990s show *Babylon 5* (1993–98) played by Walter Koenig, better known as Chekov from the *Star Trek* show and movies. The band Stereolab called one of their songs "The Stars My Destination" on their album *Mars Audiac Quintet* (1994). And so on. These outertexts are largely unremarkable, however, and they don't hold a candle to the overload of intertexts that distinguish the prose, plot, and aesthetics of the primary source.

INTERTEXTUALITY IN EXCESS

I have never read an SF novel that so meaningfully engages with the history of literature like *Stars*. It's a work of literary fiction as much as SF, which is a big reason why New Wavers and cyberpunks were drawn to it. Prior to its publication, there was very little literary élan in the genre with the exceptions of early progenitors like Mary Shelley, H.G. Wells, Edgar Allan Poe, and Jules Verne, but they weren't SF authors— the genre didn't exist in name until Hugo Gernsback retroactively called their work "scientifiction" in the inaugural issue of *Amazing Stories* in 1926, setting the SF wheel in motion. Later, a few authors took marked strides: Aldous Huxley's *Brave New World* (1932), Hermann Hesse's *The Glass Bead Game* (1943), George Orwell's *1984* (1949), George R. Stewart's *Earth Abides* (1949), and Ray Bradbury's *Fahrenheit 451* (1953) all demonstrate the sensibilities of literary fiction. Bradbury was probably the finest prose stylist among Bester's SF contemporaries, but *Stars* turned heads with its careful attention to cultural, historical, psychological, and philosophical issues as well as its use of symbolism, allegory, language, and most of all, intertextuality.

There are three primary works from which *Stars* takes its cue. First and foremost is Alexandre Dumas's *The Count of Monte Cristo* (1844). Second is Joyce's *Portrait of the Artist*. Third is William Blake's "The Tyger." Bester uses a broader stroke with Joyce. He follows the basic structure of Dumas's novel while harnessing themes and imagery from the six stanzas that comprise Blake's short poem.

McCarthy masterfully unpacks the intertextual exploits of *Stars* in "Science Fiction as Creative Revisionism," an article that elucidates Bester's literary prowess and suggests that SF actively reinterprets old forms. Here's the overarching thesis:

> Ever since Mary Shelley created *Frankenstein* out of the fruitful union of her own powerful imagination and a host of Promethean, Faustian, and

Miltonic echoes, the SF writer has often assumed the role of literary revisionist, becoming the reinterpreted of our most compelling motifs and images in terms appropriate to the scientific romance. [...] Like Mary Shelley, who allowed Frankenstein's monster to learn to read partly so that she could impose her typically Romantic reading of *Paradise Lost* upon the reader, the SF revisionist builds upon his predecessor's insights to reshape the vision and move toward a new approximation of truth. (58)

SF revisionists, then, draw from the well of the SF megatext. This is something that all SF authors do, consciously or unconsciously. That vast yet specialized code of terminology and themes cannot be evaded; setting out to write any kind of SF text inevitably engages the SF megatext, which, like the Blob, grows larger with every new text it assimilates. Authors like the creative revisionist engage the megatext more emphatically than others.

McCarthy's article was published in the early 1980s before cyberpunk had become a certified movement or at least called one by a large enough group of people (literary movements are almost always created for marketing or scholarly purposes). McCarthy mentions Olaf Stapledon's *Star Marker* (1937), which pre-dates *Stars*, and Walter M. Miller's *A Canticle for Leibowitz* (1959), which post-dates *Stars*, as examples of other novels exhibiting creative revisionism. These are valid literary SF texts, but they're exceptions to a rule that Bester tried to break.

I'm apprehensive about the notion that SF authors "often" practice revisionism vis-à-vis the scientific romance. This certainly wasn't the objective of pulp and Golden Age SF authors, and that's not what I see most authors who presume to write SF doing today. The only significant co-op that did have this objective belonged to the New Wave. McCarthy isn't wrong, but he's talking about a relatively short time period. More importantly, he doesn't give *Stars* enough credit for being a prototype for future literary work in the genre. A good deal of this work emerged in the New Wave, then threaded into cyberpunk and postcyberpunk literature in watered-down guises, especially if we consider the absurdist profusion of punk derivatives (e.g., steampunk, biopunk, splatterpunk, solarpunk, elfpunk, dieselpunk, monkpunk, etc.). Much of this fallout can be traced back to *Stars*, which is a tracing itself, a palimpsest that places (and plays with) multiple texts one atop the other. The novel changed how many readers and writers thought about SF. Bester showed us that it could be much more than adolescent schlock. Not only that—like Gully reborn, SF could be a literature of aesthetic beauty and transcendence.

For me, *Stars* is an American extension of H.G. Wells's turn-of-the-century scientific romances, namely *The Time Machine* (1895), *The Island of Dr. Moreau* (1896), *War of the Worlds* (1898), and *When the Sleeper Wakes* (1899). From a literary standpoint, much of what lies in between Wells and Bester is forgettable. McCarthy hypothesizes that *Stars* is "an intriguing instance of the operation of literary influence in an SF novel, for it is a case of genuine 'intertextuality'" (59). He doubles down on this idea by suggesting that it can be used to reread the texts it incorporates in a different light.

The impetus for *Stars* stemmed from Bester's desire to write something that appropriated plot elements from *The Count of Monte Cristo*. The protagonist of Dumas's epic, doorstopper-length adventure tale, Edmond Dantès, shapes Gully's own experience: his quest for revenge, his education in and escape from prison, his return to society as an *arriviste*, and his climactic discovery that love and empathy is stronger than vengeance. Anybody familiar with Dumas will recognize the parallel, but as "interesting as these various allusions are," says McCarthy, "they tend either to have a largely decorative effect [...] or to provide a wider context in which to judge the events of the novel" (59).

More substantive (but less noticeable) is Bester's appropriation of *A Portrait of the Artist*. Recall the revision of the nursery jingle in the last chapter of *Stars*: "Gully Foyle is my name / And Terra is my nation. / Deep space is my dwelling place, / The stars my destination" (16). This is not just the revision of the jingle that we see in the first chapter. It's also a revision of a lyric that appears in Joyce's autobiographical novel: "Stephen Dedalus is my name, / Ireland is my nation. / Clongowes is my dwellingplace / and heaven my expectation" (13). Unlike the jingle, which was presumably sung to Gully as a child, the lyric is a prank, scribbled onto the flyleaf of Stephen's geography textbook by a schoolmate making fun of him. Both, however, convey the same message and imply a quest for identity and futurity. Gully and Stephen are becoming-animals propelled by a hysterical desire to mature, transform, and escape from the nations that bind them, actually and psychologically.

Portrait of the Artist concerns the spiritual, intellectual, moral, and artistic growth of Joyce's anti-heroic protagonist from metaphorical blindness to (in)sight. Far less experimental than *Ulysses* and *Finnegans*

Wake, this profoundly affected *künstlerroman* borders on the autohagio-graphic, beginning with the title (i.e., it's not a book about an artist; it's a book about *the* Artist). Bester isn't without affect, but whatever strains of authorial ego leak into *Stars* are comparatively meager. Conversely, Gully functions more like Stephen's Unleashed Id, a fiery Hyde to the docile Jekyll of Joyce's repressed young milquetoast. Gully shares Stephen's intrinsic growth, but in a very different context. Bester extrapolates a regional, deeply personal account into the twenty-fifth century. Ireland becomes the solar system and Stephen the student becomes Gully the prole under apocalyptic auspices.

McCarthy sheds light on the symbiotic relationship between Gully and Stephen in greater depth:

> Bester's adaptation of Joyce's rhyme points toward a rather sophisticated use of the Joycean text […] Stephen [Dedalus] has inadvertently foreshad-owed both the conclusion of Joyce's novel and the emergence of Gully Foyle as the apotheosis of mankind at the end of Bester's novel. […] Stephen is at the center of the universe, [and] the path to cosmic vision begins with the individual vision of the artist. […] It is no wonder, then, that at the end of *A Portrait of the Artist* Stephen emerges as the godlike artist assuming power over "his handiwork," or that Bester should have chosen to echo Joyce's work in developing his own portrait of the artist figure as Romantic rebel, anti-hero, and godlike creator. What is most important about Bester's adaptation of a line from Joyce's work is that it implies a "reading" of *A Portrait of the Artist* through its demonstration of the Romantic possibilities inherent in the allusion. (60)

Romanticism is another noteworthy movement that correlates with *Stars*. I will say more about it in the next chapter when I discuss how Bester riffs on *Frankenstein*, an additional intertext that also relates to Blake's "The Tyger." Shelley's monster can be viewed as an extrapolation of Blake's feral, fearsome animal, with Gully drawing energy from both of these problematic creations, each of which puts morality and divinity in question.

"The Tyger" is *Star*'s dominant intertext. Blake's imagery speaks to Gully's emotional and psychological plight, and the poem's meditation on the purpose of divine creation informs Gully's conversion from rancorous everyman to rarified superman. The first and last quatrains of the poem are mirror images that form an envelope stanza. Bester uses it as an epigraph for his novel: "Tiger! Tiger! Burning bright / In the forests of the night, / What immortal hand or eye / could frame thy fearful symmetry?" (5). The refrain refers to a divine creator as well as the creator of the poem, an authorial god who bookends his poem with this "burning" question. Accordingly, Bester frames his text and calls attention to his own authorial "hand" and "eye"—which may be as problematic as his savage creations. If god is a mad scientist, so is Blake, and so is Bester.

Beyond the epigraph and UK title, allusions to "The Tyger" recur throughout *Stars*. A "reference to Blake is […] implied in every instance of the tiger theme which Bester introduces in the Prologue as part of an explanation of 'jaunting,'" writes McCarthy (61). The first invocation occurs in the prologue when Royal Society spokesperson Sir John Kelvin calls jaunting "a Tigroid Function […] associated with the Nissl bodies, or Tigroid substance in nerve cells" (Bester, *Stars* 11). Bester's most conspicuous uses of tiger imagery, however, "are the tiger-like tattoo that seems to be a mark of Foyle's rage; the enigmatic appearances of the Burning Man, a flame figure with Gully's tiger face whose form specifically recalls Blake's 'Tyger Tyger, burning bright'; and Gully's ultimate recognition that the tiger represents not only him but all of the 'driven men … Compulsive men … Tiger men who can't help lashing the world before them'" (McCarthy 61).

The Count of Monte Cristo, *Portrait of the Artist*, and "The Tyger" are all performative character studies in which Dumas, Joyce, and Blake pose questions about their individual subjects and the human condition. Bester synthesizes and science fictionalizes these performances via Gully. He doesn't stop there. As if this (self-)referential trifecta isn't enough, he pushes it further—*much* further—signifying an entire microcosm of literary precursors.

Bester's intertextuality is as pyrotechnic as his prose. Besides Swift, Dumas, Joyce, Shelley, and Blake, he pulls from the work of authors and thinkers from a variety of disciplines. Among them are (in no particular order) René Descartes, Homer, Herman Melville, William Shakespeare, Charles Dickens, John Webster, A.E. Van Vogt, Arthur Rimbaud, Stendhal, Honoré de Balzac, Robert Louis Stevenson, Charles Fort, Joyce Cary, Gerard Manley Hopkins, J.K. Huysmans, Charles Reade, Ernest Hemingway, F. Scott Fitzgerald, Ezra Pound, P.D. Ouspensky, Ali Nomad, and Charles Darwin. All of these figures have been cited by other scholars with regard to *Stars*. This list isn't exhaustive, and it doesn't include *Star*'s attention to Christian and Buddhist doctrine, but the point is clear: Bester has gone intertextually hogwild.

Authors usually deploy this allusive technique as a sleight of hand. Here it becomes an unceasing attack—more like a prolonged fistfight than a subtle, stylized flourish. What is the effect? Most conspicuously, the excess of intertexts reflects the excessive method of pyrotechnic fiction, which, for better and for worse, makes superfluity into an art form. Moreover, aside from Bester's over-the-topness, like all intertextuality, his usages enrich the experience of reading and interpreting a work of literature. But the most compelling reason has to do with the culture of *information overload* leading up to *Star*'s conception and composition.

Again I return to McLuhan. His studies of the media landscape hinged on the ways in which information overload increasingly affected subjectivity, winding us up like automatons whose agential powers are mitigated by larger portions of anxiety, panic, and dread. There were more advances in technology between World War I and II than any other foregone period in terrestrial history. By the mid-twentieth century, electronic technology was everywhere—on the streets, in homes, and in the sky—issuing from screens and speakers—forcing people to rethink how they perceived themselves and the world. The increase of households with television sets in the 1950s was transformative in itself; suddenly, people had a new way to inject the drugs of news and entertainment. McLuhan and Bester were born in the early 1910s and lived through these modern technological changes, which impacted their thinking and writing. As M. John Harrison says, "Bester was one of the first to see that *Popular Mechanics* does not free but enslave us" (26). I'm not suggesting that Bester consciously uses intertexts to critique or satirize the culture that bore him or that frames the world of *Stars*. Structurally, however, this reading works perfectly well in its historical context, and it reasserts one of the central functions of SF: to represent imagined futures in ways that make commentary on the past. That said, McLuhan and Bester are both schizoanalytic collagists, and I like the idea that their works render them the monstrous offspring of the monster of culture.

Whatever we think of Bester's intertextual aggression—like Gully and PyrE, another "Tigroid Function"—I don't take the stance of critics who think of it as mere ornamentation, affect, or flamboyance. Rather, I side with Riggenbach: "Allusion is a time-honoured literary device that has seen infrequent usage in science-fiction, Bester's or anyone else's. When Bester does allude, however, he ties his allusions so integrally to the meaning of the work that this device may be considered one of his major stylistic mannerisms" (174).

THE SLEEPERS MUST AWAKEN

In chapter 10 of *Stars*, Gully and Robin jaunte from a costume party in Shanghai to the Spanish Stairs in Rome searching for a lead that may point the way to Gully's enemies. It's New Year's Eve, and they're both dressed to the nines, "Foyle in the livid crimson-and-black tights and doublet of Cesare Borgia, Robin wearing the silver-encrusted gown of Lucrezia Borgia. They wore grotesque velvet masks" (157). Their garish Renaissance attire contrasts with the futique vogue of everybody else, who respond with "jeers and catcalls. Even the Lobos who frequented the Spanish Stairs, the unfortunate habitual criminals who had had a quarter of their brains burned out by prefrontal lobotomy, were aroused from their dreary apathy to stare" (ibid.). This brief scene not only reveals how Gully and Robin stick out like sore thumbs (an irony considering that Gully is supposed to be incognito); it also points to Bester's authorship and the (re)actions generated by the publication of *Stars*.

Building a bridge can be as divisive as it can be unifying. If we reconnoiter the twentieth century, *Stars* (the Golden Gate realization of *Demolished*'s cantilever) bridges pulp SF and modernism with the New Wave and cyberpunk, but not everybody was excited about it. I recall veteran SF and fantasy author Piers Anthony's response to my postcyberpunk novel *Codename Prague* (2009): "I am not a fan of cyberpunk, if that is what this is, don't understand it, and don't get pleasure from it. I prefer solidly plotted stories [...] I am reminded of the works of James Joyce; *Finnegans Wake* is said to be well worth the two to four years it takes to properly read it. But as I said, it's not my thing. So I'm not in a position to recommend [*Codename Prague*], but that is not at all the same thing as saying it's not competent; I suspect it's a good novel of its type." Anthony wrote this over two decades after the tackle box of the cyberpunk movement had been emptied into SF (and reality) at large. *Stars* is more linear and accessible than many New Wave and cyberpunk texts, but in its time, it confused and ostracized a lot of readers and authors, who weren't interested in that kind of newness and didn't want to be taken out of their comfort zones. In this respect, Bester struck a proverbial McLuhanesque note, his amplification equalized by amputation.

If we scrutinize the line that *Stars* draws between early and late twentieth-century SF, certain themes remain constant, like control subjects. Foremost among them is the theme of awakening, which is common to all literature, as in bildungsroman narratives like (not coincidentally) *Gulliver's Travels* and *Portrait of the Artist*. In SF, this theme traditionally emerged in utopian and dystopian tales through the vehicle of an ignorant, fish-out-of-water sleeper, dating back to late nineteenth-century novels such as Edward Bellamy's *Looking Backward* (1888), William Morris's *News from Nowhere* (1890), and H.G. Wells's *When the Sleeper Wakes* (1899). As "the nineteenth century progressed and the planet became more and more thoroughly explored, authors of utopias and dystopias began to abandon present-day lost worlds and islands as venues for their ideal societies, and instead to locate their speculations in the future [...] Almost always these speculations were framed by prologues [...] set at the time the novel was written; this frame served to introduce the protagonist who was to travel into the future and act the role of inquisitive visitor to the new world" (Clute and Langford). Thus *Star*'s flagrantly expository prologue—considered anathema by contemporary standards; immersion has long been the preferred tactic—alludes to these early SF texts while pyrotechnically satirizing the beginning of Dickens's *A Tale of Two Cities* (1859).

Bellamy, Morris, and Wells all make their protagonists fall asleep and wake up over a century later. How the protagonists remain alive for that long is attributed to ambiguous, anomalous states of deep sleep, the credibility of which neither the authors nor the readers of their day cared about—slumber was merely a way for the authors to flick their protagonists into imagined futures where they could then make commentary on those futures and point fingers at the shortcomings of their own nineteenth-century societies. Later, post-Bester SF sleepers became more surreal, metaphorical, or both, as in Kim Stanley Robinson's *A Short, Sharp Shock* (1990), Philip K. Dick's *The Three Stigmata of Palmer Eldritch* (1965), Robert Heinlein's *Stranger in a Strange Land* (1961), Russell Hoban's *Riddley Walker* (1980), M.A. Carey's *The Girl with All the Gifts* (2014), and Frank Herbert's *Dune* (1965).

Bridging the old with the new, Gully's experience falls somewhere between actual slumber and metaphoric surreality, with an emphasis on the latter. He repeatedly falls asleep and awakens to find himself in circumstances that he must adapt to and negotiate, most notably the formative trauma of the Scientific People tattooing his face after he passes out. On the whole, though, he is a figurative sleeper whose awakening hinges on moral education and the cultivation of empathy. He endures a radical shift in perception from being dumb and violent (asleep) to smart and kind (awake). It's actually a simple, childish way of enacting this theme that has more affinity with pulp than post-pulp SF. And that's precisely the point—*Stars* critiques pulp SF. Specifically, it critiques writers and readers of the pulps, trying to get them to wake up, too. Gully's journey from ignorance to enlightenment reflects the journey that Bester wants the SF community to take with him.

At the end of the novel, Gully jaunts across the world sermonizing in gutterspeak about the unlocked potential of humankind. The scene marks the penultimate stage in the transformation of his character into an übermensch, but it can also be read as a self-reflexive slap in the face. Using Gully as a mouthpiece, Bester speaks to the SF genre, defying its people to open their eyes, to stop acting like children, to unlock the potential ignored or refuted by most SF authors, editors, and publishers. *Stars*'s conclusive moral imperative has been criticized for being clichéd, sappy, and melodramatic. Again, that's the point. It's a metafictional parody of clichéd, sappy, melodramatic, boyish/boorish SF—a representation that urges us to transcend the represented content.

McCarthy equates Gully's moral evolution and near-completion with Frankenstein's monster. Like Shelley's novel, *Stars* ends on an unresolved note. "The difficulty in arriving at a moral judgment may be even greater here than in *Frankenstein*, the grandfather of all SF novels about Promethean figures. Like other types of Prometheus, Foyle is both destroyer and redeemer, Satan and Christ—not alternately but at the same time. […] Walking a tightrope between the poles of destruction and resurrection, both of which are implicit in visions of the apocalypse, Bester's conclusion is ironic in its refusal to resolve the book's paradoxes" (67). Bear this tightrope in mind as we segue to the next chapter in which I juxtapose *Stars* with *Frankenstein*, the first SF novel.

References

Anthony, Piers. "Ogre's Den: From the Desk of Piers Anthony." *HiPiers.com*. 2009. http://www.hipiers.com/09aug.html. Accessed February 18, 2021.

Ballard, J.G. *The Atrocity Exhibition*. 1970. London: Fourth Estate, 2011.

———. "Which Way to Inner Space?" 1962. *A User's Guide to the Millennium: Essays and Reviews*. London: Flamingo, 1997. 195–98.

Bester, Alfred. "Alfred Bester: The Stars and Other Destinations." Interview by James Phillips. *Starlog: The Science Fiction Universe* 128 (March 1988): 34–36, 72.

———. "My Affair with Science Fiction." 1975. *Redemolished*. New York: iBooks, 2000. 443–76.

———. *The Stars My Destination*. 1956. New York: Vintage Books, 1996.

Bier, Jesse. "The Masterpiece in Science Fiction: Power or Parody?" *Journal of Popular Culture* 12.4 (Spring 1979): 604–10.

Bishop, Michael. Preface to "In Memoriam: Alfred Bester 1913–1987," by Isaac Asimov. *Nebula Awards 23*, edited by Michael Bishop. New York: Harcourt Brace Javanovich, 1987. 22–24.

Clute, John and David Langford. "Sleeper Awakes." *The Encyclopedia of Science Fiction*. September 20, 2020. http://www.sf-encyclopedia.com/entry/sleeper_awakes. Accessed February 20, 2021.

"Foil." *The Oxford English Dictionary*. n.d. https://www.oed.com. Accessed May 11, 2021.

Gaiman, Neil. "Of Time, and Gully Foyle." *The Stars My Destination*. New York: Vintage Books, 1996.

Gibson, William. "*The Stars My Destination* by Alfred Bester." In "The Stars of Modern SF Pick the Best Science Fiction." *The Guardian*. May 13, 2011. https://www.theguardian.com/books/2011/may/14/science-fiction-authors-choice. Accessed October 28, 2020.

Harrison, M. John. "The Rape of the Possible." *Frontier Crossings: Conspiracy '87 45th Annual World Science Fiction Convention*, edited by Robert Jackson. London: Science Fiction Conventions Ltd., 1987. 26–28.

Jameson, Frederic. *Postmodernism, or, The Cultural Logic of Late Capitalism*. 1991. Durham: Duke University Press, 1999.

Joyce, James. *Portrait of the Artist as a Young Man*. 1916. New York: W.W. Norton & Company, 2007.

McCarthy, Patrick A. "Science Fiction as Creative Revisionism: The Example of Alfred Bester's *The Stars My Destination*." *Science Fiction Studies* 10.1 (March 1983): 58–68.

McLuhan, Marshall. *Understanding Media: The Extensions of Man*. 1962. Berkeley: Ginko Press, 2017.

Nicholls, Peter. "Bester, Alfred." *The Encyclopedia of Science Fiction*. March 26, 2020. http://www.sf-encyclopedia.com/entry/bester_alfred. Accessed October 23, 2020.

———. "New Wave." *The Encyclopedia of Science Fiction*. December 7, 2020. http://www.sf-encyclopedia.com/entry/new_wave. Accessed February 2, 2021.

Preiss, Byron and Howard Chaykin. "Introduction." *The Complete Alfred Bester's The Stars My Destination*. New York: Epic Comics, 1992.

Riggenbach, Jeff. "Science Fiction as Will and Idea: The World of Alfred Bester." *Riverside Quarterly* 5.3 (1972): 168–77.

Smith, Jad. *Alfred Bester*. Chicago: University of Illinois Press, 2016.

Wendell, Carolyn. *Alfred Bester*. 1982. Cabin John: Wildside Press, 2006.

Williams, Paul. "Introduction." *The Stars My Destination*. Boston: Gregg Press, 1975. x–xv.

———. "The Strange Case of Byron Preiss Visual Publications." *Journal of American Studies* 55.1 (February 2021): 102–29.

Wolfe, Gary K. "Note on the Texts." *American Science Fiction: Five Classic Novels 1956–1958*. New York: The Library of America, 2012. 813–18.

CHAPTER 4

The Frankenstein Riff

Abstract Scholarly discussions of the relationship between *Stars* and *Frankenstein* have been marginalized in favor of other intertexts. Mary Shelley's masterwork is an important point of reference. The text of *Stars* is a palimpsest beneath which lurks an underworld of other texts, and many of these undertexts are palimpsests themselves, most of all *Frankenstein*. Both novels tell the stories of charismatic monsters and meta-referentially point to the inherent mad scientism of Shelley and Bester's artistry as well as narrative itself. Bester adopts a Romantic ideal in the tradition of gothic literature that Shelley adopted for *Frankenstein* and that extends through *Stars* to New Wave and cyberpunk. He moderates an open discussion with Shelley through a multiplicity of narrative layers, including H. G. Wells's scientific romance *The Island of Dr. Moreau* and the universal motif of the monomyth.

Keywords Frankenstein · Gothic · Palimpsest · Metafiction · Romanticism

© The Author(s), under exclusive license to Springer Nature Switzerland AG 2022
D. Harlan Wilson, *Alfred Bester's The Stars My Destination*, Palgrave Science Fiction and Fantasy: A New Canon, https://doi.org/10.1007/978-3-030-96946-2_4

CALL FOR SUBMISSIONS

One of the last questions James Phillips asks Bester in the 1984 *Starlog* interview concerns the cycle of death and rebirth, a recurring topic in his work. Bester claims he doesn't worry about death. He likes the idea of rebirth, not necessarily after we die, but after we undergo strong experiences. "[W]e must always start over again," he says, "otherwise, experience is wasted. My sole motivation is to create[,] to start thinking what no one has ever thought before and out of that to turn it into literature, a painting, sculpture, or a piece of furniture, and to have a new approach that will open everybody's eyes" ("Alfred" 72). Conducted in 1984, the interview contains some of Bester's last words in print; initially publication had been slated to coincide with his Guest of Honor appearance at WorldCon in 1987, but it was delayed when he canceled because of declining health. His sole motivation spans his entire career: to make mountains out of molehills via the power of his imagination.

In this chapter, I explore how the creative impulse informs Bester's authorship and the inner workings of *Stars*. A similar impulse animates Mary Shelley's *Frankenstein*, an important intertext that has taken a back seat in scholarly discussions to Blake's "The Tyger," Dumas's *The Count of Monte Cristo*, and Joyce's *Portrait of the Artist*.

Different intertexts produce different effects. Whereas Joyce allowed Bester to plug *Stars* into the modernist project, his Frankenstein riff aligns *Stars* with a longer history of SF as well as Romanticism and gothic fiction. Additionally, it meta-narrationally aligns Bester's authorship with mad scientism, which he advocates, but not in the way that most SF authors before him enacted "madness." He aspired for a different kind of performativity that transcended conventional praxis. Extending and elevating Shelley's vision to new heights, *Stars* puts out a call for submissions to SF writers, imploring them to inject the genre with the same radical venom that *Frankenstein* used to spark it.

AN AGE OF FREAKS, MONSTERS, AND GROTESQUES

In the prolog of *Stars*, a third-person omniscient narrator recounts the future history of jaunting from the time of its originator, Charles Fort Jaunte, who discovers this self-willed, self-transporting psionic ability, opening "the frontier of the mind [...] in a laboratory on Callisto at the turn of the twenty-fourth century" (8). We begin with an instance of mad scientism, with a man creating a monster that all human beings have the power to create within themselves. Tellingly, Jaunte makes the discovery by accidentally setting fire to his work bench and himself. This produces the death-fear that makes teleportation possible. Seventy feet away from the lab bench is a fire extinguisher. Frenzied, Jaunte sees it, wants it, needs it … and suddenly, he's standing next to it.

Cut to the twenty-fifth century. The narrator describes how jaunting evolved to the point that anybody could do it by means of extreme focus as long as the jaunter has seen the destination beforehand. "Any man was capable of jaunting provided he developed two faculties, visualization and concentration. He had to visualize, completely and precisely, the spot to which he desired to teleport himself; and he had to concentrate the latent energy of his mind into a single thrust to get him there. Above all, he had to have faith […] He had to believe he would jaunte. The slightest doubt would block the mind-thrust necessary for teleportation" (11). No jaunters have ever traveled through space—the practice is restricted to planet surfaces—or gone further than 1,000 miles. There is no rationale for this figure. As with many future-historical "facts," Bester plays fast and loose, as if to bite his thumb at the rules of the SF game. But the "facts" are subsidiary. Bester's thesis is that jaunting changed human relations over the course of a century.

In the vein of classic SF, the narrator's tone is ominous, melodramatic, hard-boiled, and nostalgic. It reminisces the opening paragraph of *War of the Worlds* in which Wells's narrator reflects on the "infinite complacency" that led to mankind's "great disillusionment" (3). Bester adopts the same attitude, but with greater pomp and circumstance, explaining how jaunting inevitably led to economic strife, interplanetary war, and a profusion of mental and physical aberrations. "It was an age of freaks, monsters, and grotesques," intones his narrator, whose voice is difficult to listen to objectively, separated from my subjective idea of Bester's voice. "All the world was misshapen in marvelous and malevolent ways" (*Stars* 14).

The narrator's concern with what the "Classicists" and especially the "Romantics" think of this world pervades the prologue and points to Bester's voice more emphatically. "'Where are the new frontiers?' the Romantics cried. […] 'Bring back the romantic age […] when men could risk their lives in high adventure'" (9, 8). True to their name, these Romantics romanticize a past that had gone stale until the advent of jaunting, a tool for high adventure and a double-edged sword. "The Classicists and Romantics who hated it were unaware of the potential greatness of the twenty-fifth century. They were blind to a cold fact of evolution … that progress stems from the clashing merger of antagonistic extremes, out of the marriage of pinnacle freaks. Classicists and Romantics alike were unaware that the Solar System was trembling on the verge of a human explosion that would transform man and make him the master of the universe" (14).

Here Bester mounts his critique of SF—those "who hated it" and "were unaware of the potential greatness of the twenty-fifth century" can be perceived as old-school SF writers who hated experimental tactics and were oblivious to the untapped capacity of the genre. At the same time, Bester connects *Stars* with (pulp) adventure fiction, but primarily he invokes Romanticism, a nineteenth-century movement in the arts and literature. Romantic authors celebrated artistry and imagination, emphasized exotic locations and events, wielded sensory details like cinematic special effects, and focused on intense emotion, individual growth, and sublime states of being. *Stars* achieves all of these Romantic ideals. Bester personifies them most intensely in Gully. A certified freak of nature, his protagonist must navigate the freakshow of twenty-fifth-century life sparked by Charles Fort Jaunte's isolated, accidental, psychotic Big Bang—a pyrotechnic revolution of the self that, for better and for worse, produced a revolutionary age.

GOTHIC SCIENCE FICTION

In addition to being the most widely cited ur-text in SF studies, *Frankenstein*, like its monstrous antihero, is a stitched-together patchwork, a fusion of body parts from other genres. Shelley imports techniques and tropes from the epistolary, horror, gothic, Romantic, bildungsroman, philosophical, and literary novel.

Carl Freedman synthesizes what many other critics have said about *Frankenstein*, "the 'first' work of science fiction, or, more precisely, […] the first work in which the science-fictional tendency reaches a certain level of self-consciousness, thus enabling a line of fiction that, at least in retrospect, can be construed as the early history of science fiction proper—that is, fiction in which the tendency of science fiction is clearly dominant" (*48–49*). Equally dominant in *Frankenstein* are the tendencies of gothic fiction, a Romantic precursor with close ties to the horror genre that can be traced back to Horace Walpole's *The Castle of Otranto* (1764). Walpole blended medieval supernatural elements from the twelfth and thirteenth centuries with realist fiction of the eighteenth century, effecting a sense of uncanny terror and wonder. Half a century later, Shelley riffed on Walpole's novel and raised the stakes, creating a full embodiment of the supernatural in her monster.

Consequently, *Frankenstein* is not only the SF ur-text, but a master-work of gothic fiction and a pre-text for the cross-genre of gothic SF. In *Gothic Science Fiction: 1818 to the Present* (2015), Sian MacArthur locates the rise of the cross-genre with the first publication of Shelley's great accomplishment: "*Frankenstein* carries weight because in explic-itly exploring the potential of *actual* scientific experimentation upon humanity, Shelley is moving away from the realms of traditional Gothic and into something new, and that is the beginnings of Gothic science fiction, a sub-genre of the Gothic, recognisable by its specific interest in science, industry and technology within a gothic structure" (2).

Gothic SF conflates traits from both genres and emphasizes the "perse-cution of the innocent" resulting from an antagonist's unrealized desires (9). Such narratives are dominated by male characters and patriarchal enti-tlement. Notable motifs include immortality, the battle between good and evil, existentialism, the blurring of objectivity/realism and subjec-tivity/fantasy, and vengeful monsters. Shelley emboldens all of these motifs in *Frankenstein*, and they figure prominently in cyberpunk. *Neuro-mancer* and *Blade Runner*, for example, both tell gothically dark tales and feature monstrous creations who revolt against their creators—one in the form of an artificial intelligence (Wintermute), the other an android (Roy Batty)—not to mention that Gibson's multivalent portmanteau title signifies how *Neuromancer* jacks into (and jacks up) Romantic and SF paradigms as a new kind of (scientific) romance.

Casting a wide net, MacArthur moves from *Frankenstein* through Robert Louis Stevenson's *The Strange Case of Dr. Jekyll and Mr. Hyde* (1886) and Wells's scientific romances up to the *Star Wars* and *Dr. Who* series. She culminates in modern-day superhero comics and films, namely those featuring Batman. In the end, MacArthur says that gothic science fiction has a bright future, partly because it's among the "freest in terms of subject matter that exists today" (162), partly because it's fueled by scientific progress, which shows no signs of slowing down. I associate her use of the term "freest" with a capacity for excess. After all, gothic SF is an exercise in excess the goal of which increasingly seems to be how many stones we can pile atop a body without smashing it beyond recognition.

Classics notwithstanding, an argument could be made that *Frankenstein* carries more stones on its shoulders than any modern text in any genre.

In *Cyberpunk and Cyberculture*, Dani Cavallaro recounts additional topics shared by cyberpunk and gothic fiction: decay, obsession, disorder, transgression, helplessness, social unrest, irresolution, madness, paranoia, secrecy, and unease (xiv, xx). Cyberpunk may be the closest descendant to gothic fiction that the SF genre has ever seen. I have already traced the movement back to *Stars*, which can be traced back to *Frankenstein* through the filter of high modernism and pulp SF. In turn, *Frankenstein* stems from *The Castle of Otranto*, which siphons medieval literature. That's a timeline of over 800 years (and we could keep going, reverting to the epic sword-and-sandals fantasy of, say, the biblical Revelations and ancient Greek tragedies like Aeschylus's 458 B.C. *The Orestia*). The timeline achieves a multigeneric, metareferential climax in cyberpunk, and we can collapse all of it into *Stars*, a gravitational centerpiece for this chaotic profusion of literary styles, poses, and manic cross-pollinations.

THE AUTHOR AND THE MAD SCIENTIST

All creative writers are mad scientists, if only by aspiring to harness the power of the imagination for acutely subjective ends. In spite of its prevalence, this SF arch-cliché remains a compelling figure. Victor Frankenstein is an insufferable egomaniac, but he's far more sympathetic than subsequent mad scientists, who tend to be either unambiguously villainous or unmindful that their actions might have detrimental consequences. From Stevenson's Henry Jekyll, Wells's Alphonse Moreau, and Fritz Lang's C. A. Rotwang to Ian Fleming's Julius No, Stanley Kubrick's Dr. Strangelove, Philip K. Dick's Palmer Eldritch, Ridley Scott's Eldon Tyrell, and Michael Crichton's Henry Wu, the mad scientist has become ubiquitous to the point of normalcy; throw a dart at a dystopian SF novel or film these days and you'll probably hit one that features some manifestation or offshoot of this obsessive-compulsive genius.

Like the creative writer, the mad scientist's primary objective is just that: *to create*. More specifically, it is to create something original and shine light on the accomplishment of the creator. Unlike creative writers, however, literary and cinematic mad scientists are almost always men whose exploits illuminate masculine insecurities and anxieties. The great meta-irony that the prototype, Victor Frankenstein, was created by a woman hasn't been lost in scholarly discussions of gender dynamics.

So-called "experimental fiction" in particular certifies the mad-scientist protocol of the authors who produce it. These authors perform experiments on the "natural" bodies of conventional storytelling, vivisecting them like Moreau taking apart an animal and "Making It New." High modernist writers exemplified this practice, as did postmodern writers (e.g., William S. Burroughs's "cut-up" technique references the practice by name). *Frankenstein* is not often associated with experimental fiction, but Shelley takes considerable liberties with form and point-of-view, oscillating between reliability and unreliability, subjectivity and objectivity, letters and straight narration. She embeds multiple stories into a mainframe that imparts a narrative Russian doll. Over the years, several undergraduate students have told me that reading it can be like tumbling down a few circles of Dante's *Inferno* and then climbing back out. This schizophrenic (i.e., "mad") framework calls attention to the workings of the psyche. We don't think in organized, linear ways. We think in ever-expanding rhizomes. *Frankenstein*'s preoccupation with psychological forces is as pronounced as its preoccupation with the forces of nature and culture. Fittingly, the novel reflects the cognitive dissonance it represents in the structure of its textual body.

Within this structure, Shelley uses a variety of tactics to refine her creation and give it more personality. One of them intimately unites *Frankenstein* with *Stars*: rampant intertextuality. This was a familiar tactic used by Shelley's contemporaries. She lays it on thick, sometimes for mere ornamentation, usually with greater purpose and meaning. The subtitle contains the first and most recognizable intertext. Just as *Tiger! Tiger!* signals Blake's poem with a bullhorn, so does *A Modern Prometheus* allude to the ancient god of fire, which Shelley modernizes.

In Greek mythology, Prometheus is a notorious trickster who also dabbles in mad scientism, creating mankind out of clay, then stealing fire and giving it to mankind in order to "spark" civilization and engender the arts and sciences; as a result, he must endure eternal torment for his ambition and audacity. Victor is a Romantic version of Prometheus that interpolates him in the early nineteenth century when industrialism and advances in technology really started to change human relations and trigger anxieties about identity and community. Correspondingly, Gully, a literal and figurative Burning Man who becomes godlike, is a new Romantic (and *neuromantic*) version of Prometheus interpolated in the twenty-fifth century, a hypertechnological era where monsters like Victor's nameless creation run rampant and have become the status quo.

Shelley imbricates Prometheus with the plight of Satan and Adam from John Milton's *Paradise Lost* (1667). Her monster acquires language from reading the epic poem, which instigates his view of the world. To inaugurate the numerous drops that occur throughout the text, Shelley puts an epigraph from the tenth book of *Paradise Lost* on the title page. Spoken by Adam, the epigraph reads: "Did I request thee, Maker, from my clay / To mold me Man? Did I solicit thee / From darkness to promote me?" (3). At once human and inhuman, the monster equates himself with both Satan and Adam: "Like Adam, I was apparently united by no link to any other being in existence; but his state was far different from mine in every other respect. He had come forth from the hands of God a perfect creature, happy and prosperous, guarded by the especial care of his Creator [...] but I was wretched, helpless, and alone. Many times I considered Satan as the fitter emblem of my condition, for often, like him, when I viewed the bliss of my protectors, the bitter gall of envy rose within me" (90).

If Victor is the mythological Prometheus, the monster is Milton's Adam/Satan—and all of them are Gully. The consummate Besterman shows us "a new Adam's genesis" while exhibiting the cosmic defiance that Satan has for the Law of the Father (Hipolito 78). Prometheus and Satan share Gully's hot-tempered, hard-headed, hellbound disposition. Adam, on the other hand, the monstrous invention of God (the ultimate mad scientist), symbolizes the post-demolished, post-Fallen potential of the "stereotype Common Man," a castaway who, at the end of *Stars*, will summon a new Eden from within himself—or, in Milton's words, "a Paradise within thee, happier far" (309)—as he gazes into the Abyss like a starchild, "eyes burning with divine revelation" (Bester, *Stars* 257). Thus the monster in *Frankenstein* for whom "[e]vil thenceforth became [his] good" becomes the maker in *Stars* (Shelley 159).

Frankenstein's other intertexts include works by Homer, Shakespeare, Saint George, Lodovico Ariosto, Garcia Rodriguez de Montalvo, Cornelius Agrippa, Paracelsus, Albertus Magnus, Aesop, Volney, Plutarch, Goethe, and Xenophon. Shelley brings these historical luminaries into discussion with many of her Romantic peers, principally Charles Lamb, William Wordsworth, Samuel Taylor Coleridge, and her husband, Percy Bysshe Shelley, whose poem "Mont Blanc" provides a context for the sublime power of nature and the dangers of trying to comprehend and culturize it. As J. Paul Hunter notes, all of these intertexts "are appropriately invoked to provide comparisons of atmosphere or tonal support, and they suggest the expansive, resonant practices of reading nineteenth-century novels in a leisurely and outgoing way. Like her contemporaries, Mary engaged in allusive or intertextual practices that invited readers to notice borrowings and celebrate their own skills of knowing, noticing, and seeing the relevance" (xvi).

Intertextuality was once fairly conventional. It has less and less resonance in the twenty-first century's anti-intellectual climate. Readers and writers alike are subject to constant mediatization and canned, dumbed-down fiction that infrequently qualifies as "literature," per se. With few exceptions, today a novel is only as good as its ability to be easily adapted into a film. This wasn't the case in Bester's time, but he foresaw the cultural escarpment that we continue to slide down, and *Stars* can be read as an effort to salvage what has become a lost art—once normative, now esoteric, if not altogether alien.

Again, Shelley wasn't the first one to play games with perspective and form. Nor was she unique in the habit of (inter)textploitation. Like Bester, however, the broad, inimitable scope of her elemental excesses and categorical fusions yielded an original work that had a profound influence on subsequent authors, movements, and media.

EXPLORATIONS IN EXPERIMENTALISM

As with humor, what constitutes experimental fiction can be wildly subjective. Most readers seem to agree that Mark Z. Danielewski's postmodern ghost story *House of Leaves* (2000) is patently experimental, for example, whereas I would argue that it conforms to narrative expectations and standard plot devices, including character development. From the beginning, what Danielewski's doing and where he's going becomes evident in spite of his many textual (re)arrangements. Other readers might think a linear, conventionally organized narrative with clear parameters is experimental if the content is unfamiliar or simply "weird." Take Katherine Dunn's *Geek Love* (1989). It's not an experimental novel, by my reckoning, but whenever I teach the book, almost every student disagrees, locating Dunn's experimentalism in her central conceit: a man and woman decide to breed their own traveling freakshow by genetically altering their children's DNA and deforming them (more mad scientism!).

For me, the main component of experimental literature is newness reified by stylistic innovation. *House of Leaves* aspires to innovate style, but

Danielewski's would-be clever machinations (as well as his epistemological, academic satire and efforts to be metanarrational) are as transparent as they are predictable. In its historical context, *Frankenstein*, on the other hand, achieves genuine newness via the multigeneric and textual vivisection that *House of Leaves* wants to put into effect.

Not only was Shelley married to one of the biggest names in the Romantic movement, she came from literary grandeur: her mother and father, Mary Wollstonecraft and William Godwin, were both eminent intellectuals and writers, with Wollstonecraft, who died giving birth to her, credited as a feminist progenitor. *Frankenstein* is well-known for being conceived one night in a writing competition during the summer of 1816 between an 18-year-old Mary Shelley, Percy Bysshe Shelley, Lord Byron, and Byron's physician John Polidori to see who could produce the best ghost story. The precocious teenager originally composed a short piece. Percy convinced her to write a novel. It didn't come easy. Shelley tested different conventions, concepts, and styles, none of which she found suitable. At last, she created her own line of flight.

Despite subjective views of experimental literature, we can identify certain anchors. In popular discussions, a wealth of sources attempt to establish a comprehensive definition. An anonymous article published by *Writer's Relief*, for instance, lists the following criteria: "Not easy to read. Not escapist. Challenges tropes, genre traditions, and literary traditions. Not necessarily linear. Deliberately unsettling or even disturbing. Explores 'big' ideas. Isn't always subtle. Knowingly mixes fiction and fact. Embraces metafiction. Plays with language. Doesn't necessarily adhere to traditional prose layout. Might embrace mixed media" ("Experimental"). In another article for *Daily Writing Tips*, Maeve Maddox says that "most readers of fiction expect novels to adhere to certain conventions: at least one sympathetic character with whom we can identify and root for; a story with a clear beginning, middle, and end; a narrative style that draws us into the fictional dream; language that conforms to standard rules of syntax, meaning, and punctuation; typography that conforms to printed conventions regarding margins, etc." Literature that violates these conventions gestures toward experimentalism.

Most scholars admit that a concrete definition is difficult to nail down, and while Laurence Sterne's *The Life and Opinions of Tristam Shandy, Gentleman* (1759) is an experimentalist ur-text, literary experimentalism didn't gain traction until the modernist movement. Shelley might be viewed as a kind of pitstop between Sterne's eighteenth-century narrative inventions and the completely unhinged textploitations of Joyce, Woolf, Pound, Eliot, and Stein in particular, just as Bester might be viewed as a pitstop between pulp SF (and modernism) and the New Wave (and postmodernism). The problem with any type of artistic experimentation is that it doesn't last long—the novelty wears off quickly, especially when an author makes his or her readers work too hard, as all genuine experimental literature does. Written in formal, decorative, emotionally charged prose typical of the Romantic era, *Frankenstein* was more accessible to Shelley's contemporaries than to twenty-first-century readers, but it still smacked of the New, and nobody can discount its unique contribution not only to SF and other speculative genres but to the history of literature. Shelley trumps Bester in this respect. *Stars* is a literary novel, but it's deeply rooted in the SF genre, and there's almost no discussion of it outside of SF studies.

Frankenstein and *Stars* share many of the experimental anchors listed above. They are both viscerally unsettling and disturbing, subvert traditional prose layouts, mix fiction and fact, challenge old literary traditions, and explore "big" philosophical ideas. They also both display metafictional self-reflexivity. In *Frankenstein*, this quality lies in its Russian-doll structure. It begins with a series of letters written by explorer Captain Robert Walton to his sister. Walton rescues Victor Frankenstein as he pursues the monster across the Arctic, and Frankenstein tells him his story, which he recounts to his sister. Within Frankenstein's story, the monster tells his own story, which Walton recounts, too. There are four main texts or filters: Shelley's novel, Walton's letters, Frankenstein's story, and at the bottom, the monster's story—all of which call attention to the nature of storytelling, a fundamentally unreliable, subjective process that puts authorship in question. "Walton's exploration of the unknown is just as wide-eyed, ambitious, and unreliably utopian as is Frankenstein's quest for the secret life," Hunter writes, "and through experiments with points of view (with Walton, Frankenstein, and the Creature successively presenting their perspectives), we get both a shifting sense of authority and doubts about the reliability of authority itself" (xvii).

Stars's self-reflexivity lies in its commentary on the SF genre, such as the scene on the Spanish Stairs and the novel's climactic moral imperative. As Smith observes, Bester's metafictional enclosures were often in-jokes meant for readers in the know. For instance, the "Scientific People, whose naive worship of scientific relics in *Stars* so belies their name, [...] gently satiriz[es] what Bester saw as the all-too-human tendency of some SF writers to treat science as a magic talisman and of certain readers to accept it as such. Bester walked a fine line between parody and pastiche, poking fun at and paying homage to the SF idiom all at once" (15). Bester has been called a writer's writer, but Smith thinks he's "better understood as an uncommon variety of reader's writer. His writable approach to fiction, which took shape in his early career and peaked in the late fifties, resulted in open texts with layered, incongruous meanings that invited the reader to coproduce, even finish, his stories through active imagination. This sort of narrative metageometry made Bester's stories like proofs solvable by more than one set of steps, or games of chance in which probability weighs against odds and patterns of play" (180). In *Stars*, this metageometry reached a pinnacle, although Bester amplified it in later works, most visibly in *Golem*^{100}.

More than anything, experimental literature plays with traditional narrative formats and integrates media beyond mere words and sentences read from left to right on the page. In good experimental literature, these integrations enhance the reading experience by deepening the resonance of what would otherwise be conveyed by storytelling alone. Bester outperforms Shelley in this area, even if his experiments are limited. *Frankenstein*'s story emerges from the folds of a complex epistolary and multiperspectival network. *Stars*'s story is much more straightforward until the end when Bester introduces a succession of images and typographical effects to convey Gully's synesthesial breakdown/breakthrough.

In the fifteenth chapter, Gully finds himself "trapped in a labyrinth of twisted beams, stones, pipe, metal, and wire" beneath Old Saint Patrick's Cathedral in New York City after an earth-shaking explosion of PyrE (Bester, *Stars* 232). His clothes catch fire as molten copper pools toward him. Panicking, Gully's fight-or-flight impulse kicks in. "He was trying to escape. Like a trapped firefly or some seabird caught in the blazing brazier of a naked beacon of fire, he was beating about in a frenzy … a blackened, burning creature, dashing himself against the unknown" (233). In this extreme state of anxiety, his sensorium implodes. "Sound came as sight to him […] Motion came as sound to him. […] Touch was taste to him […] He was suffering from synesthesia, that rare condition in which perception receives messages from the objective world and relays these messages to the brain, but there in the brain the sensory perceptions are confused with one another. […] He reverted from a conditioned product of environment and experience to an inchoate creature craving escape and survival and exercising every power it possessed" (233, 234, 235).

The intensity of the situation makes Gully jaunte through space as well as time, unbridling the superheroic horseman within him. In order to better relate the experience to readers, Bester deploys typographical and imagistic patterns "to suggest altered states of perception, [Gully's] near-hallucinatory stream of consciousness" (Smith 151). These patterns range from uncanny assemblages of font and syntax to drawings of what look like crystallized flora and fauna. Just as Gully has fallen into a burning pit, so does the text fall into this high-modernist, Mad Hatter maelstrom. "Rhythmic, Dadaesque nonsense language crosses over into the more straight-forwardly narrative portions of the scene. Bester also skews the logic of dialogue attributions, assigning dialogue not only to people but to phenomena" (152).

For today's more literate readers, this kind of experimentation may come off as trite, and it doesn't work for me—these special effects momentarily *jaunte* me out of the novel's diegesis and remind me that there's an author pulling puppet-strings. The same can be said for minor flourishes like the male and female symbols that project from the names of individual Scientific People, marking their gender and, as projections, indicating how both sexes are bound to the phallus and patriarchal power. For anyone familiar with the evolution of experimental fiction *after* Bester as well as what came before him, these literary moves may not be all that exciting. But in the 1950s, few SF authors had attempted to install high-modernist techniques in their work, and what Bester did in *Stars* was fresh and original at the time, like *Frankenstein* in Shelley's time.

Experimentalism enabled Bester to give *Stars* the "fiery finish" that had frustrated and delayed its completion. The idea came to him during a conversation with a filmmaker. In a 1977 interview for *Tangent*, Bester says:

> I remember very distinctly getting into a conversation with a young Italian director who spoke about as much English as I did Italian; we had to draw pictures for each other … and we were talking about the things they would not let us write, or do, and I described to him synesthesia, which I had wanted to do for a long time as a television script because it's a visual thing, and how furious I was because they'd never let me touch it. It was too original, nobody would understand, the budget wouldn't understand, all of that nonsense; and while I was describing it to this director it hit me like Christ Jeezus on a raft! *That* is the finale of the book! *That's* what holding you up, old Alf! You don't know *where* you're going. *Now* you know where you're going—go man, go!

Bester's discovery solidified *Stars*'s Make-It-New ethos and was well-received by most readers, who hadn't really seen this sort of innovation in genre SF before. Anything that breaks rules and veers from the familiar is prone to irk people, though, and some readers didn't like it. Despite her belief that *Stars* is a stroke of genius, Leslie Flood characterizes Bester as a mad creator who lets his monster run astray: "The problem now is to bring this conglomeration to a satisfactory finale. Bester once more indulges his original idiosyncrasy in describing thought-sensations, by way of a typesetter's nightmare, and the crucial scene in St. Patrick's Cathedral is magnificently done. Then somehow the author loses his grip on his creation. Foyle's stimulus for revenge has been removed, and he is given an out-of-character realization of the problems facing mankind over PyrE and imminent space-jaunting for all [...] This is the author blatantly intruding after letting his fanciful characters parade their phantasmagoria through most of the book" (127).

Flood locates the intrusive aspect of Bester's experiment in what follows the "typesetter's nightmare." This takes place in the final, sixteenth chapter where the narrative reverts to standard form and Gully converts into a didactic vicar. Like the anonymous fifteenth-century morality play *Everyman*, the Common Man now realizes that good deeds are the only thing that will save him from himself, so he jaunts around the world preaching to the masses. Flood is right about Bester's intrusion, but she doesn't account for its metafictional satire. Moral allegories dominated SF until the New Wave broke that tradition over its knee. The further we go back in time, the more SF moralism we encounter—through pulp SF, through the scientific romances of H. G. Wells, all the way back to *Frankenstein*, an allegory about the dangers of violating the laws of nature. Chapter sixteen satirizes this tradition by (re)making Gully in the image of the SF megatext's go-to protagonist. Then, in the final paragraphs, Gully waits to be reborn—to transcend that tradition and become something better, something *outré*.

Regardless of Flood's critique—and my own critique, for that matter—Bester's synesthesial typography and imagery complements the pyrotechnic circus of wonders that distinguishes the novel from start to finish.

"None Escape": Star's Palimpsest

The text of *Stars* is a palimpsest beneath which lurks an underworld of other texts, and many of these undertexts are palimpsests themselves, most of all *Frankenstein*. Both novels' intertextuality signifies their undertextuality and the ways they overwrite their predecessors. As such, Bester moderates an open discussion with Shelley through a multiplicity of narrative layers. A substantive layer belongs to H. G. Wells's scientific romances. Tracings of *The Island of Dr. Moreau* are markedly visible. Bester's overlay binds Gully, Victor, and the titular vivisectionist to one another.

No mad scientist is born in a vacuum. He is who he is because of his insecurities and anxieties, which were instilled in him by past experiences and racial, patriarchal entitlement (in addition to being predominantly male, most SF mad scientists are white). If I had to choose a governing quality, it would be narcissism. Bourgeois and egocentric, Victor Frankenstein is absolutely consumed with himself and wants his name in lights. He "desires to be the first in the field in the regeneration of life and he will not settle for anything less. His fervent desire for fame and glory combined with his innate arrogance and ambition make for a temperamental and destructive personality that is only partly redeemed by his repentance at the end of the text" (MacArthur 27).

Victor loves his family and friends, but when his monster starts killing them off, it's as if the monster is destroying parts of his maker's ego, which is oddly resilient. Victor bounces back from grief too quickly. An expert at disavowal, he foregrounds what he wants over what is real, often mistaking the two. After promising to make the monster a bride, for instance, he decides to travel around Europe for two years with his friend Henry Clerval, pretending that everything is fine, or will be fine, or has always been fine—whatever serves his emotional and psychological needs. Finally, he begins to construct the bride, then trashes the body before completion in a fit of umbrage. "[T]rembling with passion, [I] tore to pieces the thing on which I was engaged. The wretch saw me destroy the creature on whose future existence he depended for happiness, and, with a howl of devilish despair and revenge, withdrew" (Shelley 119). Victor knows how things will play out, but again, he disavows the monster's threat—"I shall be with you on your wedding night" (121)—and he convinces himself that the whole escapade is a figment of his imagination. "Indeed, as the period approached, the threat appeared more as a delusion, not to be regarded as worthy to disturb my peace, while the happiness I hoped for in my marriage wore a greater appearance of certainty, as the day fixed for its solemnization drew nearer, and I heard it continually spoken of as an occurrence which no accident could possible prevent" (138). Here and elsewhere, Victor suffers from the central narcissistic fallacy that truth is a matter of desire, that objectivity is the plaything of subjectivity.

Gully might be more narcissistic than Victor, but he's not as smart, even after Jiz educates him in Gouffre Martel. Samuel R. Delany rightly calls him "an unformed lump of elemental violence" (27). Furthermore, Gully incarnates Victor as much as his monster, although some criticism posits that the monster is Victor's doppelgänger—the unbound dark side of Prometheus, as the novel's subtitle indicates. Whereas Shelley draws clear distinctions between the creator and the creation, however, Bester collapses these distinctions into Gully, a mad scientist who experiments upon his own body, reinventing himself as the cyborg harlequin Geoffrey Fourmyle of Ceres. Granted, Gully didn't perform the experiment on himself; he hired the chief surgeon of the Mars Commando Brigade to turn "him into an extraordinary fighting machine. Every nerve plexus had been rewired, microscopic transistors and transformers had been buried in muscle and bone. [...] The operation [...] had transformed half his body into an electronic machine" (128, 129). But Gully's pathology dictates terms. The surgeon who technologizes him is merely a disposable Igor mentioned in passing. As a self-experimenter, he reminisces Wells's Invisible Man, who imitates Stevenson's Dr. Jekyll. All three mad scientists try to remake themselves into something new and better. Ironically, only Gully, the dumbest of the bunch, succeeds.

The freaks, monsters, and grotesques that populate *Stars* weren't created in a vacuum either. There are plenty of other mad scientists running around the solar system, and Gully isn't the only maniac who formulates his own monstrous identity.

The madness of the Scientific People sets Gully on the path of destruction that leads him to redemption. The Māori mask that they tattoo on his face is the most visible marker of his monstrosity. Facial tattoos aren't that big of a deal these days, but seventy years ago, they were transgressive. Bester extrapolates that transgression into the twenty-fifth century for his 1950s readers. Even after Gully has the tattoo surgically removed, he can't shake its ghost, which flares up like stigmata whenever he loses his temper, a constant reminder that he, like Victor's creation, is a "wretched devil"

(Shelley 68). The tattoo becomes a rule of law that he must obey in order to remain incognito as his enemies pursue him. Presteign, Dagenham, and Y'ang-Yeovil have never seen him and can only identify him via the tattoo, so he must keep his emotions in check; nobody can escape themselves, after all. This subject-position alludes to the Beast Folk of *The Island of Dr. Moreau* who must follow the rule of law delivered by their creator. As if in church, they regularly gather together in the jungle to listen to the Sayer of the Law, responding to his gospel with this mantra: "None escape" (Wells 62).

In Chapter 6, Bester explicitly channels *The Island of Dr. Moreau* into Harley Baker's Freak Factory. Dr. Baker is an unassuming medical practitioner who moonlights as a mad scientist from a three-story lab in Trenton, New Jersey, where he "create[s] monstrosities for the entertainment business and refashion[s] skin, muscle, and bone for the underworld" (Bester, *Stars* 92). Gully hires him to remove his tattoo. In the basement of the factory is a zoo "of anatomical curiosities, natural freaks and monsters bought, hired, kidnapped, abducted. Baker, like the rest of the world, was passionately devoted to these creatures and spent long hours with them, drinking in the spectacle of their distortions the way other men saturated themselves with the beauty of art" (95). Baker's mania mirrors that of Dr. Moreau. A research biologist, Moreau retreats from London society to a remote island and establishes his own zoo, vivisecting animals and making them into people that can talk and walk on hind legs. Like Baker, Moreau is interested in the "beauty of art" that his experiments bestow in spite of the immense pain that he inflicts upon his subjects, but the pain is subsidiary to both narcissists' pursuit of scientific and aesthetic grandeur.

Wells's novel extends *Star*'s palimpsest by invoking the tradition of SF island narratives dating back to proto-SF texts such as Thomas More's *Utopia* (1516) and *Gulliver's Travels*, but "Wells's debt to these traditions in the story," says John S. Partington, "is perhaps slighter than his debt to more contemporary issues like nineteenth-century advances in biological science and related discussions concerning ethics, civilization, and the role of religion in society" (1103). Likewise is Bester indebted to mid-twentieth-century advances in science and technology, just as Shelley is indebted to early-nineteenth-century advances. Mad scientists tend to live in imagined futures, but as with all SF, their exploits critique the time period in which their authors created them. *Star*'s palimpsest reveals a wealth of embedded, multi-coded SF intertexts and themes alongside social commentaries. Bester piles all of these plateaus one atop the other, rendering *Stars* an intricate lens that allows us to peer deeply into the well of the SF megatext. On every page, we can't escape from the history of SF.

The Monomyth

Stars, *Frankenstein*, and *The Island of Dr. Moreau* all exhibit qualities of the monomyth or hero's journey wherein protagonists go on an adventure that takes them from familiar into unfamiliar territory. As fish out of water, they suffer trials and tribulations that result in some kind of transformation or at least a change in perspective. The monomyth is a ubiquitous formula. In *The Hero with a Thousand Faces* (1949), Joseph Campbell, spellbound by psychoanalysis, attributes the origin of the term to Joyce's *Finnegans Wake* and traces it back to biblical, Buddhist, Greek, and other ancient lore (343). He says the monomyth is a universal motif that extends to the far reaches of human society and culture. To my mind, the motif works best in speculative genres that can push the limits of what constitutes "unfamiliar territory," but Campbell is right to say that it exists everywhere.

Donald Palumbo hypothesizes that *Stars* implements the monomyth like no other SF novel before it. "Although perhaps most remarkable for its exhaustive elaboration of the monomyth's pivotal death-and-rebirth motif," he writes, *Stars*

> also depicts antihero Foyle as possessing most of the qualities of the monomythic hero [...] Moreover, the monomyth's theme, transcendence (which its death-and-rebirth motif symbolizes), is unmistakably this landmark science fiction novel's theme as well; and the monomyth's fractal pattern-within-pattern internal structure is likewise echoed in *The Stars My Destination*'s recurring things-within-things internal structures, which are evident in the disguises-within-a-disguise donned by Foyle as he pursues an agenda-within-an-agenda as well as in the onionlike layers-within-layers structure of the various presumed and actual reasons why *Vorga* passes Foyle by when he is marooned aboard the *Nomad* (the novel's seminal event), of the various answers to the question of who gave the order to do so (the novel's most explicit mystery), and of the various presumed and actual reasons why he is being pursued by Outer Satellites' agents as well as by Presteign's agents and Inner Planets' Central Intelligence (the novel's crucial revelation). (334)

I have discussed *Stars*'s layerings in terms of intertexts and undertexts. Palumbo shows how the monomyth designates even more layerings, and in support of his thesis, he itemizes a remarkable *eleven* symbolic deaths and rebirths that Gully endures on his monomythic path to awakening and enlightenment. Most involve metaphorical descents into Hell (e.g., escaping through Gouffre Martel's underground gorge) and/or bodily mutilation (e.g., the sensation of being "flayed" and "devoured" in the cyberspatial Nightmare Theater [Bester, *Stars* 61]). Whatever the case, "these symbolic deaths and rebirths all signify the transformation of his psyche and of the nature of his relationship to reality, just as Campbell argues that the monomyth's pervasive death-and-rebirth motif in itself represents metaphorically those many moments of transition from one phase of life to the next that occur in everyone's experience—and not, literally, life after death" (Palumbo 343).

Victor Frankenstein and the narrator of *The Island of Dr. Moreau*, Edward Prendick, endure similar cycles of death and rebirth. For example, Prendick finds his way to Moreau's island after a shipwreck in the southern Pacific Ocean. Starving, he drifts for eight days in a dingy with several other passengers who sink into derangement, attack one another, and fall overboard. Thereafter, Moreau's assistant Montgomery passes by in a schooner, rescues Prendick, and nurses him back to health. Here is this monomythic hero's first symbolic birth. There are others in the novel, but nowhere near on the scale of *Stars*, one of "the most popular and aesthetically successful science fiction novels ever written, in large part, due to its sophisticated integration of the monomyth's theme and fractal internal structure into its more superficial use of the monomyth's anatomy of the hero and overall plot" (334). Echoing Prendick, Gully is first born from the womb of a ship. Then Bester proceeds to demolish and redemolish him like a banshee.

At the beginning of this chapter, I talked about Bester's lifelong interest in the topic of death and rebirth, an enabling factor in his career-spanning quest for "a new approach that will open people's eyes." Nowhere in his entire cannon does he manifest this topic like he does in *Stars*. Gully chronically dies and returns to the womb to be born again and again and again. Victor's monster despises being a creation. So does Gully, but he craves it like a drug, and he can't stop doing it. Only in the womb does his rancor abate. Which is why, at the end of *Stars*—back in

Nomad, in "the womb of the locker" (258), dreaming a good dream, his Romantic journey from Innocence to Experience complete—he's never been happier. For all intents and purposes, he will live to die another day.

REFERENCES

Bester, Alfred. "Alfred Bester: The Stars and Other Destinations." Interview by James Phillips. *Starlog: The Science Fiction Universe* 128 (March 1988): 34–36, 72.

———. "An Interview with Alfred Bester." *Tangent* 6 (Winter 1977): 25–33. https://tangentonline.com/interviews-columnsmenu-166/classic-alfred-bester-interview. Accessed March 14, 2021.

———. *The Stars My Destination*. 1956. New York: Vintage Books, 1996.

Campbell, Joseph. *The Hero with a Thousand Faces*. 1949. Novato: New World Library, 2008.

Cavallaro, Dani. *Cyberpunk and Cyberculture: Science Fiction and the Work of William Gibson*. New Jersey: The Athlone Press, 2000.

Delany, Samuel R. "About Five Thousand, One Hundred and Seventy-Five Words." *SF: The Other Side of Realism*, edited by Thomas Clareson. Bowling Green: Bowling Green University Press, 1971. 130–46.

"Experimental Fiction: What Is It and Who's Publishing It." March 3, 2019. https://writersrelief.medium.com/experimental-fiction-what-is-it-and-whos-publishing-it-13e1fefe507b. Accessed March 3, 2021.

Flood, Leslie. "Book Reviews." *New Worlds* 17.50 (August 1956): 126–28.

Freedman, Carl. *Critical Theory and Science Fiction*. Hanover: Wesleyan University Press, 2000.

Hipolito, Jane and Willis E. McNelly. "The Statement Is the Self: Alfred Bester's Science Fiction." *The Stellar Gauge: Essays on Science Fiction Writers*, edited by Michael J. Tolley and Kirpal Singh. Victoria: Norstrilia Press, 1980. 63–90.

Hunter, J. Paul. "Introduction." *Frankenstein; or, The Modern Prometheus*. 1818. New York: W.W. Norton & Company, 2012. ix–xviii.

MacArthur, Sian. *Gothic Science Fiction: 1818 to the Present*. New York: Palgrave Macmillan, 2015.

Maeve, Maddox. "What Is 'Experimental' Fiction?" *Daily Writing Tips*. n.d. https://www.dailywritingtips.com/what-is-experimental-fiction.   Accessed March 3, 2021.

Milton, John. *Paradise Lost*. 1667. New York: W.W. Norton & Company, 2020.

Palumbo, Donald. "The Monomyth in Alfred Bester's *The Stars My Destination*." *The Journal of Popular Culture* 38.2 (2004): 333–68.

Partington, John S. "*The Island of Dr. Moreau* by H.G. Wells (1986)." *The Greenwood Encyclopedia of Science Fiction and Fantasy: Volume 3*. Westport: Greenwood Press, 2005. 1102–104.

Shelley, Mary. *Frankenstein; or, The Modern Prometheus*. 1818. New York: W.W. Norton & Company, 2012.

Smith, Jad. *Alfred Bester*. Chicago: University of Illinois Press, 2016.

Wells, H.G. *The Island of Dr. Moreau*. 1896. New York: Bantam Dell, 2005.

———. *War of the Worlds*. 1898. New York: Bantam Dell, 2003.

CHAPTER 5

Architectures of Psyche, Power, and Patriarchy

Abstract A distinct social division of classes typifies *Stars*'s twenty-fifth century, as does an egregious misogyny and underlying racism. All three issues come to bear in the persona of Gully Foyle. Throughout the novel, he slowly transcends these proverbial constructs of culture, which comment on the ethics of the SF genre as well as Bester himself, who is a product of his own patriarchal culture and SF's endorsement of it. Bester's fascination with Freudian psychology threaded into much of his writing and came to a crux in *Stars*, scaffolding character desires (i.e., inner space) and technoculture at large (i.e., outer space). His attitudes toward class, gender, and race are at once progressive and regressive. On the whole, however, he was more evolved than his contemporaries and made strides toward greater equality despite his own construction and entitlement as a white male author.

Keywords Power · Patriarchy · Class · Race · Gender

D. Harlan Wilson, *Alfred Bester's The Stars My Destination*, Palgrave Science Fiction and Fantasy: A New Canon, https://doi.org/10.1007/978-3-030-96946-2_5

OVERVIEW

In this chapter, I discuss issues related to class, gender, and race, focusing on (ab)uses of power and patriarchy. A distinct social division of classes typifies Bester's imagined future, as does an egregious misogyny and underlying racism, even though "more than a century of jaunting had so mingled the many populations of the world that racial types were disappearing" (Bester, *Stars* 153). All three issues come to bear in the persona of Gully Foyle. Throughout the novel, he evolves and transcends these proverbial constructs of culture, which comment on the ethics of the SF genre and Bester's own cultural construction. I will begin with some attention to how Freud impacted his authorship. To varying degrees, Bester's ideas about psychological clockwork spilled into every other aspect of *Stars* and magnified his perception of literature, art, ideology, and identity.

THE SCIENCE FICTION OF SIGMUND FREUD

Freud's sizable oeuvre is thoroughly science fictional. When I read his books, the experience is no different for me than reading an SF novel.

Most readers and scholars don't think of Freud as an SF author, but his quasi-scientific, cognitively estranging, inner-spatial explorations reflect core SF values and objectives, and his theories about the nature of desire and the workings of the psyche remain influential SF touchstones. Philip K. Dick and Barry N. Malzberg, for example, both owe a debt to Freudian ego psychology and paranoia, with Malzberg even (re)making him into a character in *The Remaking of Sigmund Freud* (1985). The mind is still relatively unknown territory, and as Brian Stableford and David Langford point out, the "absence of convenient models of the mind (whether based on physical analogy or purely mathematical) means that [it] remains much more mercurial and mysterious than the atom or the Universe, in spite of the fact that introspection appears to be a simple and safe source of data." We know as little about the far reaches of inner space as we do outer space. To this day, psychology is fertile ground for extrapolation. Freud in particular is an SF idea-machine.

The SF megatext would look different without Freud, who created the monster of psychoanalysis from the underdeveloped body parts of other clinicians, and whose original innovations outplay what most SF writers fail to accomplish themselves. Of course, Freud wasn't trying to be an SF writer, let alone a mad scientist. He thought he was writing nonfiction even as he conjured one uncanny novum after another (including *Das Unheimliche* itself). He has been disparaged over the years because his extrapolations turned out not to hold water. Like the SF writer, however, his books and case studies are works of art, and many of them contain perfectly applicable techniques for negotiating the psychopathology of everyday life regardless of the bourgeois, patriarchal entitlement that often irradiates his tone, rhetoric, and overall persona. As feminist scholars have observed, texts like *Dora: An Analysis of a Case of Hysteria* (1905) can be read as a comedy of errors in which a surrogate father tries and fails to control a young girl who won't have it, resisting his attempts to compartmentalize and "fix" her desires. Freud was a product of his cultural context. At the same time, like Bester, he was more evolved than his contemporaries and made strides toward greater equality despite himself.

Bester's love of Freud and psychoanalysis is no surprise. Both innovated their respective fields and put a premium on the power and application of the imagination. Bester's Freudian impulse dates back to the first act of his career and was partly responsible for his second turn from the SF genre when he met John W. Campbell, Jr. for the first time to talk about the publication of "Oddy and Id" in *Astounding*. Enchanted by L. Ron Hubbard's *Dianetics* (1950), Campbell made him excise the Freudian allusions from his story, convinced that Hubbard's "modern science of mental health" was a superior alternative to psychology. Over lunch, he even asked Bester to read parts of *Dianetics* and encouraged him "to use the principles [...] to purge his mental blocks and trace his emotional traumas back to the very womb, a request that left Bester somewhere between dismayed and bemused" (Smith 5). Bester wanted the sale, so he followed orders. The story was published as "The Devil's Intention" in 1950. The following year, when it was reprinted in *The Best Science Fiction Stories: 1951*, Bester had carte blanche to do as he pleased, and he reverted to the original manuscript and title.

The encounter with Campbell didn't do much to uplift Bester's spirits, especially considering that he "had returned to SF in search of creative freedom, and the editor had greeted him with a heavy-handed attitude that reminded him of his discouraging experiences with radio and television producers" (79). He rallied and started selling stories elsewhere, adorning his work with psychological trimmings and fixings. A self-proclaimed "worshiper of Freud" (Bester, "Introduction" 243), his devoutness came to a head in *The Demolished Man*, which is scaffolded by

Freudian psychology and hinges on the Oedipus complex. Charles Platt
has said that this scaffolding falls flat, calling it "disappointingly glib and
shallow" (215). I tend to agree. In *Stars*, Bester finds his stride, weaving
Freud's ideas into the novel with greater precision and a lighter touch.

Bester designs his characters from a Freudian perspective first, then
applies other points of view as he shapes them. Gully is the paradigm—
his identity is just that: an *id*-entity—but all of Foyle's foils are cut
from the same cloth. The "freaks, monsters, and grotesques" that run
rampant through the novel emote from Freud's concept of the id. "Bester
champions man's reason but often shows the id triumphant," says Tim
Blackmore. "This accounts for the dark, often desperate tone of his
stories. [...] Bester strives for a balance between rationality and unreason,
between hate and love. [His] respect for the id's forces doesn't prevent
him from generating mindscapes, incredible (rational) worlds created by
the ego and superego" (102). But the ego and superego are marginalized
by the dominance of the id, an assemblage of uncoordinated instincts that
both defines freaks and implicates humans. "Bester thrives on the issue of
what distinguished freaks from humans. Sensitive to the Freudian implications, [he] often suggests that it is the freak (the id) which makes man
human. His playful language reveals a fascination with all the dangerous
but wonderful powers man may possess" (103–104). Gully's multivalent
mask is an insignia of this dynamic, "a warning to humans about the beast
within, the wild, unreasoning id" (116).

In *Stars*, psychological praxis isn't simply a means of, say, developing
greater self-awareness or combatting depression. It is embedded into the
fabric of daily life. When Presteign hires Saul Dagenham to interrogate
Gully for the location of *Nomad*, for instance, the former nuclear scientist
tortures him with Nightmare Theater and Megal Mood. The first technique "had been an early attempt to shock schizophrenics back into the
objective world by rendering the phantasy world into which they were
withdrawing uninhabitable" (Bester, *Stars* 61). Nightmare Theater is a
proto-cyberspatial realm in which prerecorded, macabre scenarios play out
on the screen of Gully's psyche as if they were his own while Dagenham
grills him about *Nomad*. It's one of many Hells that Gully must negotiate
as he is "pursued, entrapped, precipitated from heights, burned, flayed,
bowstringed, vermin-covered, devoured," but he doesn't break—he just
keeps repeating his vengeful mantra, "*Vorga*" (ibid.).

Megal Mood stems from an early therapeutic initiative "for establishing
and plotting the particular course of megalomania" (62). Foreshadowing

the mnemonic holidays of Dick's "We Can Remember It for You Whole-sale" (1966) and Paul Verhoeven's *Total Recall* (1990), this technique attempts to convince Gully that he is not Gully but Geoffrey Fourmyle of Ceres, the id-entity he unconsciously adopts as his alter-ego in the second part of the novel. Posing as "Dr. Regan," an actor tells Gully that his memory of himself as a low-grade spaceman is false. It's not an implant. Rather, he fell into alcoholism and lost his sense of self. "You became convinced you were not the famous Jeff Fourmyle," says Regan. "An infantile attempt to escape responsibility. You imagined you were a common spaceman named Foyle" (64). Gully doesn't believe it. In order to "recapture the true memory," he must "discharge the old. All this glorious reality is yours, if we can help you discard the dream of the spaceman" (ibid.). Regan wants Gully to reconstruct "this false memory," beginning with his escape from *Nomad* (ibid.). For a moment, he bends, but again, he doesn't break. He's too tough, too resolute, more id- than egocentric.

Nightmare Theater and Megal Mood are interesting but super-fluous Freudian refrains. In their absence, little would change: they mainly convey Gully's mental stamina. Jaunting, on the other hand, is a psychological aberration that defines *Stars*'s interplanetary, war-torn, hypertechnologized society.

In and of itself, jaunting is a ridiculous idea that aligns Bester with pulp SF more than any other facet of the novel. It requires concerted suspen-sion of disbelief. Perceived through the lens of Freudian SF, however, jaunting qualifies as a viable novum.

Originator Charles Fort Jaunte gets his forenames from early twentieth-century American writer Charles Fort, who coined the term *teleportation*. Jaunte is a scientist, but his "discovery" of teleportation does not result from some kind of experiment gone wrong, as in so many mad-scientist narratives. It results from the fear of burning to death. Countless people who existed prior to Jaunte have harbored this acute stress response on similar and heightened levels, dating back to early humans running away from hungry leopards and hyenas. For some inex-plicable reason, it makes Jaunte teleport. In the prologue, Bester maps out an ambiguous history, hinting that this "natural aptitude of almost every human organism" is an evolutionary leap, an effect of tapping into the deeper, unused hollows of the brain (10). It probably has something to do with advanced technologies, too. Bester makes use of other, unreliable media to recount the history, such as a "most unsatisfactory explanation" by a Jaunte School publicity representative, who explains: "When people teleport, they also teleport the clothes they wear and whatever they are strong enough to carry" (ibid.). This convenient "perk" may be more ridiculous than jaunting itself, but it simplifies things for the author. Assuming jaunting were possible, it would make more sense that only people's organic matter would teleport—like Kyle Reese traveling through time in *The Terminator* (1984)—but then Bester would have to account for characters putting on new clothes every time they did it.

Reluctantly, Arthur D. Hlavaty acquiesces to *Stars*'s pulpy introduction, saying that the novel begins

> in the way one must never begin a science fiction novel: with a lecture on the book's main Nifty New Thing, a form of teleportation called jaunting. He gets away with it (at least with me) partly because his unnamed omniscient narrator is as much fun to listen to as Lorenzo Smythe [Robert Heinlein's first-person protagonist in *Double Star* (1956)]. The whole book is like that: a tightrope walk over many pitfalls with the author simultaneously racing and pirouetting and never completely falling off. Randall Jarrell famously remarked that a novel is a lengthy work of fiction that has something wrong with it, but Bester abuses the privilege.

Fair enough, but Hlavaty fails to recognize the prologue's self-awareness. A literal and symbolic flight of fancy, jaunting is a metafictional jab at the silly artifices of pulp SF. And it's not a passing or glossed jab. Bester effectively sustains the artifice from the prologue to the final chapter while he calls attention to the absurdity of Nifty New Things that preceded it in other SF texts.

Fear gives birth to jaunting. Over time, users learn to control the stimulus, psychokinetically relocating themselves from point A to point B through the vehicle of blind faith so long as they possess foreknowledge of their destination and don't try to teleport off-planet. The dawn of the Jaunte Age sets the stage for the social, cultural, and ontological landscape of *Stars* as well as for Bester's extrapolation of psychological tenets into a diegesis that is concerned as much with inner space as outer space. He takes most of his cue from Freudian SF, but he also draws from other sources. Hipolito and McNelly propose that Jung is the key to understanding both *Stars* and *Demolished* even though "Bester has never set out to write a novel which would embody Jungian principles" (90), and in his monograph on Bester, Smith discusses the spiritual psychology that informs *Stars*, citing Ali Nomad's *Cosmic Consciousness: The Man-God Whom We Await* (1913) and P. D. Ouspensky's *Tertium Organum* (1912), the latter of which divides consciousness into four forms that chart Gully's development. In broader terms, Fiona Kelleghan states: "A majority of Bester's stories are concerned with the themes of captivity and release, and a great many of his characters spend time in prisons or psychiatric wards. [...] His reliance on such related themes as darkness and the threat of madness reveals his interest in prisons as the site of psychological catalysis, and he dramatizes the psychology of escape and the results of release, which may be epiphanic or disastrous" (351).

Gully's physical imprisonment in Gouffre Martel after he fails to destroy *Vorga* complements the various cognitive and symbolic imprisonments that define his character as a slave to the Freudian death-drive. His desire to return to the womb is palpable, ubiquitous. In fact, Bester depicts Gully as a womb addict, born from the womb of *Nomad* where he returns in the end after passing through a multi-uterine labyrinth. His external mask emblematizes his inner womb-monger, as Neil Gaiman divulges: "The tiger tattoos force him to learn control. His emotional state is no longer written in his face—it forces him to move beyond predation, beyond rage, back to the womb, as it were. (And what a sequence of wombs the book gives us: the coffin, the *Nomad*, the Goufre Martel, St. Pat's, and finally the *Nomad* again.) It gives us more than that. It gives us: Birth. Symmetry. Hate" (x). All of this inner-spatial architecture not only lays the groundwork for Bester's superheroic, superpyschotic anti-hero but for the power dynamics that distinguish his civilization, at once a throwback to the Victorian era and a projection of mid-twentieth-century ideological apparatuses into the future.

FROM THE ABYSS TO THE MOUNTAINTOP: CLASS RELATIONS

Class divisions and capitalist morality configure the society of *Stars*, marginalizing the masses and privileging an upper echelon of stereotypical patriarchs and salon-hopping bourgeois socialites. Gully the prole occupies the bottom of the barrel. Presteign the artistocratic Neo-Victorian roosts on the tightly sealed lid. Everybody else exists within the bookends of their social statuses. In these terms, the novel sees Gully actuate a Marxist-like uprising where he vies against his bourgeois superiors. By the end, he has transcended capitalist notions of good and evil after a concerted attempt to set humanity on a new, would-be utopian path where everybody gets along, works together, shares responsibilities, and so on. This is another SF artifice, objectively impractical but metafictionally practical. SF stems from the utopian tradition in its "impulse toward change" (Vint 19), but with few exceptions—Kim Stanley Robinson's *Pacific Edge* (1995) may be one—the concept of utopia has become as silly as jaunting beyond its allegorical implications and its capacity to make social commentary. In Bester's hands, the utopian initiative satirizes heavy-handed representations of this silliness by offering a potential "happy ending" to the dystopia that harrows Gully and his twenty-fifth-century peers. Additionally, the gesture toward utopia completes Gully's Nietzschean climb from the abyss to the mountaintop of the social order. And when the sleeper awakens, he will have leapt off the mountaintop, soared into the ether, and escaped the system—a final Freudian wish-fulfillment fantasy.

Bester appears to have patterned twenty-fifth-century society after a mid-twentieth-century English model where class divisions were more pronounced than in America. This model preoccupied J. G. Ballard throughout his career and climaxed in *High-Rise* (1975). The novel depicts a literal and figurative uprising of stratified English aristocrats, professionals, and workers who live together in a near-future tower-block building. Rather than a gesture toward utopia, it ends in a way Ballard felt was more realistic: in chaos, with the residents who survive regressing to survival mode (including cannibalism). Ballard's high-rise can be viewed as a microcosm for Bester's dystopia without the culminating agential meta-fantasy and the pedantic moralization about the human condition.

In *High-Rise*, dormant tensions between classes swim to the surface and lead to warfare. In *Stars*, warfare is part of society from the outset of the Jaunte Age, which ruined the tenuous but stable socioeconomic system. "Until the Jaunte Age dawned," says the prologue's narrator, "the three Inner Planets (and the Moon) had lived in delicate economic balance with the seven inhabited Outer Satellites: Io, Europa, Ganymede, and Callisto of Jupiter; Thea and Titan of Saturn; and Lassell of Neptune. The United Outer Satellites supplied raw materials for the Inner Planets' manufactories, and a market for their finished goods. Within a decade this balance was destroyed by jaunting" (Bester, *Stars* 13). Trade exchange collapses, and the "economic war […] degenerate[s] into a shooting war" between the Inner and Outer Planets (14). The war exacerbates default class divisions and perpetuates "the marriage of pinnacle freaks" oblivious to "the cold fact of evolution […] that progress stems from the clashing and merger of antagonist extremes" (ibid.). Against this backdrop, Bester introduces Gully, the prole to end all proles.

Bester tempers the narrator's sturm-und-drang tone as he transitions from the prologue to the first chapter. Stranded on the incapacitated spaceship *Nomad* between Mars and Jupiter, Gully struggles to maintain sanity and questions why the "goddamn gods" have forsaken him (15). The first sentence equates him with Jesus on the cross: "He was one hundred and seventy days dying and not yet dead" (ibid.). *Nomad* is Gully's cross, the name of which he will soon bear on his flesh when the Scientific People tattoo it onto his forehead. The chapter is a character sketch that establishes Gully's motive for vengeance and defines the contours of his working-class status, emotional disposition, and messianic potential. I talk about religious connotations in my last chapter. For now, it suffices to say that Jesus was also a prole victimized by his proto-bourgeois masters for his socialist doctrines. Some political and theological historians claim Jesus was the first communist.

The narrator enumerates Gully's defining characteristics as follows: "Mechanic's Mate 3rd Class, thirty years old, big boned and rough[,] the oiler, wiper, bunker man; too easy for trouble, too slow for fun, too empty for friendship, too lazy for love" (16). His official Merchant Marine record indicates that he has no education, no skills, no merits, and no recommendations. Comments from the personnel department further indicate that he is a "man of physical strength and intellectual potential stunted by lack of ambition. Energizes at minimum. The stereotype Common Man. Some unexpected shock might possibly awaken him, but Psych cannot find the key. Not recommended for promotion. Has reached a dead end" (ibid.). Bester foreshadows Gully's awakening through the administrative apparatus of "personnel," consumer-capitalism's all-seeing watchdog. From the start, he contextualizes Gully in economic terms, solarizing this context with a religious corona that references the protagonist's embryonic godliness and the capitalist system's godlike stranglehold on mankind.

When *Vorga* passes by *Nomad*, his response is visceral, feverish, primal. In the lower-class gutter tongue, he gripes: "You leave me rot like a dog. You leave me die, *Vorga*. […] I get out of here, me. I follow you, *Vorga*. I find you, *Vorga*. I pay you back, me. I rot you. I kill you, *Vorga*. I kill you filthy" (22–23). For Gully, *Vorga*'s negligence is an upper-class snub, something he has encountered his entire life, but now his life is on the line, and the snub "precipitat[es] a chain of reactions that would make an infernal machine" out of him (23).

Much of the plot involves Gully's vengeful quest for *Vorga* and the parties responsible for giving the order to abandon him. The ship belongs to Presteign, whose mononymous name looks like "prestige" and symbolizes his class status while functioning as a stand-alone badge of honor. The "g" in Presteign is silent, though, so phonetically the name sounds like "pristine," indicating the corruption of something once pure and good (for the clan leader as well as his daughter). When a representative from the Internal Revenue Department calls him "Mr. Presteign," he corrects the mistake: "There are thousands of Presteigns [...] All are addressed as Mister. I am Presteign of Presteign, head of house and sept, first of the family, chieftain of the clan. I am addressed as Presteign. Not 'Mister' Presteign. Prestiegn" (46). Bier adds that the name is a "cover riddle," a "composite for the fantasied *reign* of a Prestone, first of equals among the 'Colas' and 'Buicks' and 'Kodaks' in that frigid plutocratic future" (605). As I mentioned in my first chapter, many clansmans' monikers affiliate them with commodities. These "brand names" deepen their affectation and entrenchment in a class system that elevates and pathologizes them.

The clan/class consciousness of *Stars* is a throwback to the Victorian era that upholds bourgeois codes of patriarchy and manners. This is one of several cultural reversions effectuated by jaunting, a McLuhanesque amplification that goes hand-in-hand with amputation. Another amputation produced by the Jaunte Age is the dissolution of communication systems, as "it was far easier to jaunte directly to a man's office for a discussion than to telephone or telegraph" (Bester, *Stars* 42). We mainly learn about the dynamics of clan life through Presteign, who reifies his power with amputations like "an antique telephone switchboard" because society is "[d]evoted to the principle of conspicuous waste" (ibid.), which is to say, the detritus of history marks him as an upper-class subject. And the more detritus one has, the more powerful one's image becomes. Hoarding is a form of cultural currency.

Presteign is a stock villain, a clichéd Rich White Guy with a stiff upper lip whose image and superfluities matter as much as the size of his bank account. In a movie adaptation, he would likely have an affected posh English accent to complement his thoroughly colonial mindset. "Iron gray, handsome, powerful, impeccably dressed and mannered in the old-fashioned style, Presteign of Presteign was the epitome of the socially elect, for he was so exalted in the station that he employed coachmen, grooms, hostlers, stableboys, and horses to perform a function for him which ordinary mortals performed by jaunting" (45). He also owns "carriages, cars, yachts, planes, and trains" (46), an anomaly in the Jaunte Age where on-planet transportation technologies have become outmoded. Presteign does not jaunte—it's beneath him. He hasn't jaunted in forty years, and he frowns upon everybody who does it. Eschewing this amplification is a way for social climbers to exhibit their success. "As men climbed the social ladder, they displayed their position by their refusal to jaunte. The newly adopted into a great commercial clan rode an expensive bicycle. A rising clansman drove a small sports car. The captain of a sept was transported in a chauffeur-driven antique from the old days, a vintage Bentley or Cadillac or a towering Lagonda. An heir presumptive in direct line of succession to the clan chieftainship staffed a yacht or a plane" (45).

The hundreds of Mr. Prestos that Presteign owns further reifies his affluence. Mr. Prestos are identical androids surgically tailored after the "kindly, honest" Abraham Lincoln to "instantly inspire affection and trust" in people who shop at the retail stores that they manage (47). Like Bester and Dr. Baker, Presteign is a mad scientist, but he's not interested in art or invention; social and economic standing dictates the flows of his creative desires. Bester doesn't dwell on Mr. Prestos or bind them to the plot. As an allusion to the emotionally conditioned automatons of Huxley's *Brave New World*, they function as plugs into the SF megatext while developing Presteign's character. Ultimately, they are more detritus, but unlike Presteign's telephone, they implicate futurity rather than history.

Credits are the mode of currency in *Stars*, another pulp SF cliché that more or less reflects the dollar, pound, euro, etc. Edward Bellamy may have been the first author to use credits in *Looking Backward*, but it became more common in pulp SF of the 1930s and 1940s, with the 1934–1935 serialization of Campbell's *The Mightiest Machine* in *Astounding* being a progenitor. The focal currency for the novel's plot, however, is a load of platinum bullion worth approximately twenty million credits. Unbeknownst to Gully, *Nomad* had been transporting this load to a Mars Bank on Presteign's behalf to settle a debt. Presteign, Dagenham, and Y'ang-Yeovil use the bullion as an excuse to try to extract the whereabouts of *Nomad* from Gully. What they're really looking for is PyrE, another piece of cargo on *Nomad* that Gully doesn't realize was there until much later. Once he discovers who Presteign is, an inborn class resentment fuels Gully's vengeance and prompts him to create a new identity that rivals his enemy's resources and persona.

To Presteign, Gully Foyle is a "common sailor. Dirt. Dregs. Gutter scum" (47), and he resents the fact that this lowlife stands between him, his money, and his apocalyptic warhead. Gully's existence in itself insults his Neo-Victorian dignity. Geoffrey Fourmyle of Ceres, however, is super rich and puts Gully on Presteign's socioeconomic pedestal. As the ringleader of the "grotesque entourage" Four Mile Circus and an overblown Shakespearean clown, he breaks Presteign's rules of etiquette, but his wealthy upstart status trumps his bad behavior.

Gully builds Geoffrey's assets on the foundation of the bullion he retrieves from *Nomad* on the Sargasso Asteroid at the end of the first part of *Stars*. In other words, he builds his alter-ego on the foundation of Presteign's capital and image, embodying the ancient adage that *to know your enemy, you must become your enemy*. On the surface, Gully's vengeance is emotional. Beneath the surface, it's a matter of overcoming his proletariat construction. "I teach you the superman," Nietzsche crows in *Thus Spoke Zarathustra* (1883). "Man is something that should be overcome. What have you done to overcome him?" (41). Gully responds to this question first by becoming somebody else, then by molting the skin of all of his identities, transcending construction and incarnating the übermensch. He beats Presteign by deconstructing Presteign, reconstructing himself, and calling attention to the illusory nature of the capitalist powers that created both of them as social, cultural, and economic subjects. The womb of the tool locker that he returns to in the final chapter is a version of the womb-cave that Nietzsche's Zarathustra exits at the end of his book-length sermon, which concludes with this line: "Thus spoke Zarathustra and left his cave, glowing and strong, like a morning sun emerging from behind dark mountains" (336). This is the state we leave Gully in as J♂seph and M♀ira watchfully await his awakening, a rebirth that will allegedly see him "glowing and strong," free from the class consciousness that incited such anxiety, insecurity, and blind aggression in the id-entity that he has overcome.

Foyle's Female Foils: Gender Relations

In my first chapter, I talked about the resonance of Gully's surname and some of the literary foils denoted by "Foyle." The complexity of this pun extends to the four female characters that contribute to the protagonist's development and accentuate the nuances of his evolving identity: M♀ira, Robin Wednesbury, Olivia Presteign, and Jisbella "Jiz" McQueen. All of these names signify their personas directly or indirectly. In this section, I discuss the relationship between Gully, these women, and dominant power structures. First I'll say a few words about the overall treatment of gender in *Stars*.

Whereas Bester's outlooks on gender relations were more progressive than the majority of his SF contemporaries, there are problems with the way he represents those relations and has articulated them in interviews and articles. Consider this excerpt from "Science Fiction and the Renaissance Man": "[W]omen, as a rule, are not fond of science fiction. The reason for this is obvious … at least to me. Women are basically realists; men are the romantics. The hard core of realism in women usually stifles the Cloud Nine condition necessary for the enjoyment of science fiction. When a woman dreams, she extrapolates reality; her fantasies are always based on fact. […] And the writers who appeal to them are those writers whose inwardness reflects an attitude about love, marriage and the home that is attractive to women" (418–19). As if these silly generalizations aren't enough, he goes on to make distinctions between the nature of male and female desire: "Unlike women, [men] can't find perpetual pleasure in the day-to-day details of living. A woman can come home ecstatic because she bought a three-dollar item reduced to two-eighty-seven, but a man needs more. […] Life is enough for most women; most thinking men must ask why and whither. In England men have the pub for this. […] Here in the States the thinking man has nothing" (421). Such distinctions were not uncommon in Bester's era, and he didn't catch any flak for making them. It was a man's world, and until the New Wave, SF was written almost exclusively by male authors for male readers. Needless to say, such views would not go over well in the twenty-first century (or, incidentally, the twenty-fifth century).

Gender relations in Bester's fiction are not as simplistic, embarrassing, or ripe for standup observational comedy as the author's personal attitudes, although they are strictly binary and heteronormative. Rape is a recurrent theme. Sometimes it's mentioned in passing, as in "Fondly Fahrenheit," when Vandaleur speculates that his psychotic android may have raped a child. Sometimes it's in our faces, as in the novel *Tender Loving Rape*, which Bester wrote in 1959 and wasn't published until over thirty years later as *Tender Loving Rage* after Charles Platt suggested a title change (Smith 164). Gully is the most hostile, reprehensible rapist of all. He rapes Robin to gain power and control over her, and he almost rapes M♀ira trying to escape the Sargasso Asteroid, tearing off her nightgown, then binding and gagging her with it. Nearly every encounter he has with women ends badly. As an Unleashed Id, Gully owns this behavior, and Bester doesn't condone it explicitly or implicitly. On the contrary, Gully's actions refer back to Bester's interest in Freudian masculinity and aggression.

The Besterman quivers with a violent urge that's waiting to snap like a bear trap. "Bester's characters, though they become aware of themselves precisely because of it, see no gap between the desired and the possible. Put them next to one another, straight away they begin to whisper, 'Together we could rape the universe!'" (Harrison 27). Ironically, the Besterman does not truly become himself until he has demolished himself. For Gully, rape is a tool of the prole that must be overcome. Zarathustra summons his powers from inner space, from the intellectual and imaginative "free spirit" within him, not by externalizing his aggression; the übermensch has surpassed the demands of the body. Still, there is something deeply disturbing about the recurrence of rape in Bester's oeuvre and in *Stars*. It may be a sign of his times, but it's no less troublesome, and scholarship on his work has collectively glossed over the issue.

Bester has been critiqued for downplaying and objectifying women. Platt admits:

> Bester is aware of his relative lack of empathy for his female characters (who are almost always beautiful, unthinkingly dedicated to the male hero, and altogether delightfully ineffectual). He says he is principally interested in writing about male characters, and 'I don't believe in love as a motivation at all. I dislike love stories intensely.' Hence the simplification and codification of most of the love relationships in his work. It is probably his greatest weakness although, of course, it is a weakness shared with almost every other science fiction writer working in the 1950s and before. (219)

Wendell concurs, saying that Bester's women "often are stereotypical females clinging to their men" (17), but stronger types start to emerge in *Stars*. Jiz, for example, is not an objectified pulp bimbo, but a tough, streetwise roughneck whose "attraction to Gully is not schoolgirl romanticism but adult lust" (ibid.). Wendell concludes that the "difference between the women of earlier works (the 1950s) and those of the later (the 1970s) may well result from the time frame itself and its effects on Bester's perception and awareness. In fact, Bester seems far less the male chauvinist than his contemporaries of the 1950s who produced a literature that did not stereotype the female because it did not often include her" (ibid.).

As with rape, Bester criticizes male chauvinism (among other antagonistic behaviors) via representation. An exemplary case in point is how clanswomen must be kept in purdah to "protect" them from rogue jaunters who may steal their virtue. In Muslim and Hindu societies, purdah is a religious and social practice that compels women to live in various states of seclusion and cover their bodies so as not to incite male desire. The practice enables men to control women. "You don't know what jaunting's done to women," Jiz tells Gully in Gouffre Martel. "It's locked us up, sent us back to the seraglio," an Italian term for the segregated domestic quarters of wives and concubines in an Ottoman household (Bester, *Stars* 74). Jiz describes seraglio as a "harem. A place where women are kept on ice. After a thousand years of civilization [...] we're still property. Jaunting's such a danger to our virtue, our value, our mint condition, that we're locked up like gold plate in a safe" (ibid.). She laments that there's nothing women bound to the unevolved laws of men can do. They can't work, and they have no autonomy.

While Jiz, Robin, and Olivia find some kind of agency from their patriarchal overlords, M♀ira does not. This is ironic in that the Scientific People, who have their own laws and beliefs, perceive themselves as more advanced than the interplanetary freakshow from which they have isolated themselves, and yet M♀ira's shackles outweigh her female peers. Her name says something about this irony. It's an anagram for Māori, but it also references the biblical Mary, setting her up for the conclusive nativity scene where she and J♂seph loom watchfully over baby Jesus/Gully in his manger/locker. M♀ira is not Gully's mother, though. The Scientific People marry her to him after they recover Gully from *Nomad* in the second chapter, and when he returns to the Sargasso Asteroid in the last chapter, she delights that her husband has come home to her. All male Scientific People "must marry every month and beget many children" (30). The contours of their New Age culture are nebulous at best; all we learn is that they have combined religious and pseudoscientific principles, namely the opposing forces of Christianity and Darwinism. The "science" of the Scientific People is really just patriarchy in disguise, and M♀ira is more enchained than Gully's three other would-be help*meats*, with the female symbol that extends from the o in her name reifying her subjection. If she has any agency at all, it relies on Gully's transcendence (i.e., if her man becomes Zarathustra and breaks the chains of social construction, maybe she can hitch her wagon to his star).

As a foil, M♀ira shows us how Gully's psychological and emotional disposition moves from one polar coordinate to another. He begins a violent tiger; he ends a mindful starchild. M♀ira is the least developed female character, but his brief encounters with her frame this transition.

Jiz is a much rounder character, and Gully is her Eliza Doolittle, an empty vessel that she fills with the power of knowledge. They become lovers until he abandons her on the Sargasso Asteroid after retrieving the safe from *Nomad* with the PyrE and bullion in it, but she mainly functions as a life tutor for him. Her agency from patriarchy is criminality, which is why she ends up incarcerated in Gouffre Martel. Jiz fled her home and became a master robber, carving out her freedom and individuality with every new heist. Gully can read and write, but he's still a gutter-product of his lower-class upbringing. The daughter of an architect, Jiz received a formal education and knows intimate details about the prison. With an eye to breaking out, she teaches him what she knows as well as how to speak, think, and act properly so that he can find the *Vorga* crew. "No more bombs," she says, "brains instead" (75).

Like M♀ira, Jiz's name references a biblical figure, Jezebel, the biblical queen and wife of King Ahab. Strong and serpentine, Jezebel undergirds Jiz, who has an erratic, push-and-pull relationship with Gully. One moment, she rebukes Gully and puts him in his place; the next, she melts into his arms. Their interactions are "always passionate, a mixture of fury and retaliation that generally ends in sex" (Wendell 32). Later, she and Dagenham fall in love, but her role as a foil is over. Gully is the nucleus of the gendered code that animates *Stars*. Interpellated by that code, Jiz becomes superfluous after she edifies Gully and he discards her. With Gully, she is a subject—subjected by patriarchy at large, subjected by Gully himself. Post-Gully, she is pure object, with nothing left to offer this bildungsroman novel about the development of one man's self-awareness.

Robin is the yin to Jiz's yang, innately good-natured, not virulent. Her name invokes Robin Redbreast, the "bird" (British slang for girl) that tried to help Jesus by plucking a thorn from his temple during his crucifixion in the post-biblical folktale. Wendell says she "serves as both victim of the tiger and teacher to the student. Without doubt, Robin is the most innocent and vulnerable of [Gully's] women, the defenseless bird pounced on by the vicious tiger" (30). Her psychic powers compliment her intelligence and cultural savvy, only these powers handicap her. "[S]he was a telesend, a one-way telepath. She could broadcast her thoughts to the world, but could receive nothing. This was a disadvantage that barred her from more glamorous careers, yet suited her for teaching. Despite her volatile temperament, Robin Wednesbury was a thorough and method-ical Jaunte instructor" (Bester, *Stars* 35). As with Jiz and Gully, she might benefit from some therapy for anger management, but almost every char-acter in *Stars*, male or female, has a tiger inside of them and exists on the razor's edge of anxiety: it's the nature of their monstrous, wartime civilization. The title *Tiger! Tiger!* doesn't just point at the protagonist. It incriminates his world and everybody in it.

Robin is a teacher by profession, and her reeducation of Gully in the second part of the novel expedites what Jiz started in the first part. Gully blackmails Robin into being his guide through the Dantesque circles of upper-class society on his quest for revenge. He uses her as a ventriloquist, navigating social situations with her telepathic instructions. For example, when Geoffrey Fourmyle makes his debut at a New Year's Eve ball, Robin helps him intermingle with fellow party-goers who speculate about him. As is often the case with representations of telepathy or thought-processes in fiction, Bester uses italics to denote her mental utterances.

> "Fourmyle? The clown?"
> "Yes. The Four Mile Circus. Everybody's talking about him."
> "Is that the same man?"
> "Couldn't be. He looks human."
> Society clustered around Fourmyle, curious but wary.
> "Here they come," Foyle muttered to Robin.
> "*Relax. They want the light touch. They'll accept anything if it's amusing. Stay tuned.*"
> "Are you that dreadful man with the circus, Fourmyle?"
> "*Sure you are. Smile.*"
> "I am, madam. You may touch me."
> "Why, you actually seem proud. Are you proud of your bad taste?"
> "*The problem today is to have any taste at all.*"
> "The problem today is to have any taste at all. I think I'm lucky." (140–41)

And so on. Jiz teaches Gully language; Robin enables him to use language. Bester objectifies both women by intermittently describing their physical beauty, but unlike Jiz, Robin maintains valence until close to the end when she pulls Gully out of his synesthesial delirium, a penultimate stage in his transformation. Moreover, "Robin's desire for vengeance, her determination to destroy Gully [for raping and blackmailing her], leads to her own salvation and redemption—love and mercy for the enemy" (Wendell 31). Just as Bester makes SF New, so does Gully make himself New. Neither Robin nor Jiz do it for him. They give him the know-how he needs to accomplish newness. At times, they both foil (i.e., frustrate) his plans, but ultimately, they foil (i.e., facilitate) the growth of his character.

If M♀ira frames Gully's transformation, Jiz initiates it, Robin expedites it—and Olivia completes it. Latin for "olive tree," her first name suggests peace and harmony. It's a hoax. Olivia belies her good-willed signature.

The idea that monsters are made and not born readily applies to Gully, whose tattooed cyborg body reflects the social and cultural forces that made him into a technologized tiger. Olivia is forged by social and cultural forces, too, but from the opposite end of the class spectrum, from the context of the aristocratic *elite* rather than the proletariat *deleted*. Nonetheless, her anger and resentment rival Gully's, and she is born a monster, "a glorious albino. Her hair was white silk, her skin was white satin, her nails, her lips, and her eyes were coral. She was beautiful and blind in a wonderful way, for she could see the infrared only, from 7,500 angstroms to one millimeter wavelengths. She saw heat waves, magnetic fields, radio waves, radar, sonar, and electromagnetic fields" (Bester, *Stars* 44). Olivia is the classic blind seer with an enhanced capacity for (in)sight. Coupled with her aberrant yet enticing physicality, Gully wants her more than anybody else. She's a freak like him, a tiger like him, angry at the world because of her disability. Her whole life, she felt cheated and helpless. "They should have killed me when I was born," she tells Gully. "Do you know what it's like to be blind ... to receive life secondhand? To be dependent, begging, crippled?" (210). She likes the interplanetary war because she finds beauty in other people's suffering. Her yearning for revenge is as strong (if not stronger) than Gully's. This "pair of monsters" is a match made in Hell (ibid.).

Olivia only appears five times in the novel, but she is the most important foil. Wendell offers these insights about her portrayal and connection to Gully:

> Olivia makes more famous villains pale by comparison. [...] [S]he is described each time in imagery that emphasizes her hardness, her lack of

humanity: a "statue of marble and coral" (chapter 3); "a Snow Maiden, an Ice Princess with coral eyes and coral lips" (chapter 11); "a marble statue … the statue of exaltation" (chapter 11). Always, she is cold, hard, unyielding. Her appearance and her handicap have isolated her from humanity until she has become a monster (her father's excessive protection of her has no doubt added to the situation). Her statuelike appearance suggests her marble heart; her blindness may be symbolic as well as literal: she simply does not see other people in her own "private life" (chapter 14), as she calls it. Olivia and Gully's meeting in the garden reveals their mutually inhuman passions. He starts to rescue Jiz, then Robin, but chooses, finally, to look for Olivia. […] Olivia provides the mirror for Gully Foyle: she is blind, but he sees himself in her, and the horror of that vision recreates the man. (33, 34)

Gully falls in love with Olivia because he sees himself in her as much as he sees someone entirely removed from himself. They're both Unleashed Ids, full of piss and vinegar, but they're from different worlds, with different life experiences, and Olivia is his diametric opposite in terms of image (as an albino), sex (as a woman), and class (as an aristocrat).

Some scholars have explored gender dynamics in *Stars* in theoretical terms. Hipolito and McNelly read Jiz, Robin, and Olivia through the filter of Jungian psychoanalysis, hypothesizing that, symbolically, "each woman character in *Tiger! Tiger!* represents versions of the anima which in Foyle […] has been utterly overshadowed by the dominant *animus*-tiger; Foyle's improving response to the women in his life symbolises his improving relationship to the *anima* within himself. As William Blake expresses it in 'The Tyger,' […] the Tiger is balanced by the Lamb" (81). In her monograph on Bester's oeuvre, however, Wendell offers the best overall commentary on the tiger's "lambs" of any scholarship I have read, but I think she lets Bester off the hook too easily. It's true that Jiz, Robin, and Olivia are stronger and more nuanced than most other SF female characters that predate them, but their value hinges on their association with Gully. Like dutiful housewives, their ability to make Gully a better man is what counts. In the house of Bester, once they have accomplished this goal, they have nothing left to offer.

We don't know what will happen once the reborn Gully sheds his tiger stripes for phoenix feathers. This is the case with all Bestermen: they arrive at the threshold of awakening, but they never go all the way. To go all the way would be another story, and that story wouldn't involve a Besterman, who is a becoming-man, not a newborn or completed man. A harem of enablers authorize Gully's becoming; the purdah that afflicts the twenty-fifth century of *Stars* also afflicts the development of the novel's protagonist. We could read this scenario as Bester meta-referentially suggesting how such a fraternity of gender relations needs to be overcome in literature. More likely, he's catering to a male readership, who might appreciate complex representations of women, but who, like Bester, are chiefly interested in the world, ways, and primacy of men.

Toward a Vanishing Point: Race Relations

As with class and gender, Bester underlines issues of race in *Stars*. He foregrounds Robin's blackness, and during Gully's hunt for his enemies, we learn that, as I mentioned earlier, "[m]ore than a century of jaunting had so mingled the many populations of the world that racial types were disappearing" (Bester, *Stars* 153). On our approach to the Vanishing Point, white privilege, entitlement, and patriarchy still live large, with the Presteign clan evoking the Ku Klux Klan, but *Stars* demonstrates more racial diversity and recognition than the SF novels and stories of Bester's generation. According to the entry on "Race and SF" in *The Encyclopedia of Science Fiction*, "[i]n the 1950s and early 1960s the mere appearance of an ethnic-minority character in a positive role was faintly unusual, with the exception that Native American ancestry was remarkably common in spacemen and other sf heroes" (Langford). As one can imagine, prior to the 1950s, non-white and ethnic-minority characters were comprehensively marginalized and portrayed in a negative light, and if we go back to foundational SF texts by, say, H. G. Wells and Jules Verne, the whiteness is blinding. Along these lines, reading *Frankenstein* is like staring at the sun.

Bester's efforts toward a representation of positive race relations are more successful than his efforts toward gender relations, even if that positivity is largely an effect of miscegenation and there being less differences in skin color and general appearances between people in the twenty-fifth century. The subtext here is that, in order to move beyond racial prejudice and accomplish acceptance (and ideally apathy), we must get rid of physical variance altogether. History proves again and again that "civilized" human beings hate difference among themselves and will kill each other to nullify it. But if everybody's different (i.e., if everybody is a freak, a monster, and a grotesque) does that hatred abate or cancel itself out? Or does it become more pronounced and emphatic? In *Stars*, the former seems to be the case. Bester does not volubly comment on or satirize race relations, but he does construct an allegory that puts white privilege in question by encoding his characters.

Race, gender, and class only exist because we authorize the illusion of their actuality. They are extremities of the monster of culture, and we are their collective creator, yet another iteration of the mad scientist who can't stop making and remaking and manipulating them. The most powerful of these extremities is class. Race and gender have wreaked unspeakable havoc over the course of human history. The havoc wreaked by class, however, casts a shadow on all of the suffering that has been induced by any other material ideology or cultural construction. *Stars* suggests that what outlives the past cannot defeat the future. Class dominates the status quo, and gender and race (in order of affect) operate under its umbrella. In the latter case, both the social order and the art of narrative overlay this power structure, as Samuel R. Delany notes in "The Mirror of Afrofuturism": "[T]he social and biological barriers to communication are overcome by the ability to learn new social codes that blur racial ones, even as those barriers are reduced to purely aesthetic enrichment during the course of the condensation of its epic plot" (184). Bester's attention to style and story pushes his ideas about race in the direction of disposable pulp SF novums that are more for ornamentation than meaningful orchestration. Nevertheless, Bester's attention to racial codes has more clout than mere glitz and gadgetry.

In his article, Delany implies that Bester encrypts Jiz, Robin, and Olivia with color. "Jisbella McQueen, an underworld thief [...], is a fellow prisoner with Gully in Gouffre Martel and helps him break free. Her color is red. Robin Wednesbury is a black woman teacher who is a one-way telepath, who can only project her thoughts rather than read someone else's. [...] Olivia Presteign is the albino daughter of a far-future billionaire [...] who is blind to ordinary light but sees the world through infrared illumination alone" (175). Jiz's redness presumably signifies her fiery temperament and has nothing to do with race. I wouldn't put it past Bester to code her as red for being Native American—recall that *The Computer Connection* was serialized as *The Indian Giver* in the mid-1970s—but she isn't; she's white. Robin and Olivia, on the other hand, are distinguished by their skin color, but Delany doesn't say what their pigmentation connotes. We can read Olivia's whiteness as a reflection of her class status, allying her with her father's brand of white Neo-Victorian patriarchy, which is innately pathological and choleric; in her case, race points to class, and vice versa. The purpose and function of Robin's blackness is not so clear and deserves a bit more thought.

Delany does not critique Bester or *Stars*. He critiques the SF category of Afrofuturism, arguing that it is essentially anything anybody wants it to be and not a real category at all. In his eyes, the only thing needed to invoke an Afrofuturist narrative "is black characters in the future, whatever the race of the writer" (173). Therefore, Robin is an indisputable Afro-futurist character and a precursor to the "newest new-wave trajectory" of feminist black science fiction that Marleen Barr delimits in *Afro-Future Females* (2008), a definitive anthology of criticism and stories (xii). But so what? Theoretically, what is gained by making her black? Is it simply a gesture toward diversity of characterization? Bester gives a major role to a black woman. That's an innovation for the 1950s, but it seems like her blackness should do more, even in its historical context.

Delany is too reductive and dismissive; he's from an older SF guard, and it shows in his article. In *Afrofuturism: The World of Black Sci-Fi and Fantasy Culture* (2013), Ytasha L. Womack submits a more compelling, accommodating viewpoint. She defines Afrofuturism as "an intersection of imagination, technology, the future, and liberation" (9). Citing a talk by art curator and Afrofuturist Ingrid LaFleur, she adds: "Afrofuturism [is] a way of imagining possible futures through a black cultural lens, […] a way to encourage experimentation, reimagine identities, and activate liberation" (ibid.). Robin can be regarded in these terms. In many ways, her experience reminisces the African-American slave oppressed by white authority—none more than Gully, a white man who abuses her physically and psychologically while coercing her into (telepathic) slave labor on his behalf. Ironically, Gully's slave, who becomes his upper-class mouthpiece, is smarter and better educated than him. Moreover, despite his abuse and the enmity it causes her, Robin helps her master to the very end, saving him from himself.

Robin suffers from something like Stockholm syndrome, a term coined in the 1970s for how abductees come to revere their abductors as a means of psychological and emotional agency from oppression. In his autobi-ographies, Frederick Douglass alludes to this condition when he discusses how slaves brag about their masters to other slaves. "When Colonel Lloyd's slaves met the slaves of Jacob Jepson," he writes in *Narrative of the Life of Frederick Douglass* (1845), "they seldom parted without a quarrel about their masters; Colonel Lloyd's slaves contending that he was the richest, and Mr. Jepson's slaves that he was the smartest, and most of a man. Colonel Lloyd's slaves would boast his ability to buy and sell Jacob Jepson. Mr. Jepson's slaves would boast his ability to whip Colonel Lloyd. These quarrels would almost always end in a fight between the parties, and those that whipped were supposed to have gained the point at issue. They seemed to think that the greatness of their masters was transferable to themselves" (23).

I equate this variety of Stockholm syndrome with the Freudian ego-defense mechanism, a form of hysteria induced by overwhelming circumstances. As such, Robin's subservience to Gully facilitates the *overcoming* of his old, degraded self and the *becoming* of a new, transcendent overman. She shows us that Gully must not only transcend the limits of being a violent prole and misogynist, but an entitled white patriarch. She also shows us how strong her character is. No matter how many times this white man beats down this black woman, she always gets up. Not only that, she teaches her white oppressor how not to be a victim of his whiteness. Under these auspices, Robin is an incarnation of Frederick Douglass himself.

The Civil Rights movement officially began two years before the publication of *Stars* in 1954 with the passing of Brown vs. Board of Education, which declared racial segregation in public schools unconstitutional. Bester probably wasn't thinking about Gully and Robin in terms of a power-relation between master and slave. In all likelihood, his inclusion of a black main character is meant to demonstrate how, 500 years in the future, race doesn't matter as much as it used to. But he was surely aware of Civil Rights and the plight of African-Americans, and I'd say he was as sympathetic to these causes as a privileged white man of his era could be. As with many of Bester's aesthetic choices, his depiction of Robin is both flawed and fruitful, a throwback and a leap forward, regressive and progressive—just like the freakified culture and community of *Stars* as a whole.

At a more systematic level, *Stars* doesn't explain what "racial types disappearing" entails. What the landscape might look like on the other side of the Vanishing Point is even more difficult to picture. Not much is said about racial types beyond this statement. Kellegan declares that *Stars* "features a black woman and Chinese man as major characters; race relations are healthy in Bester's future" (1273). Are they healthy, though? What does Kellegan mean by healthy? Everybody's angry and antagonistic about something in this book. Is it simply that race has taken a back seat to more incendiary, provocative issues? People haven't figured out how to get along in this future. Bester's twenty-fifth-century society hates itself just as much as (if not more than) his own twentieth-century society, which, in the early 1950s, was still raw and reeling from World War II.

The Chinese man that Kellegan mentions is Central Intelligence Captain Peter Y'ang-Yeovil, "a lineal descendant of the learned Mencius [who] belonged to the Intelligence Tong of the Inner Planets Armed Forces. For two hundred years the IPAF had entrusted its intelligence work to the Chinese who, with a five thousand-year history of cultivated subtlety behind them, had achieved wonders. Captain Y'ang-Yeovil was a member of the dreaded Society of Paper Men, an adept of the Tientsin Image Makers, a Master of Superstition, and fluent in the Secret Speech. He did not look Chinese" (Bester, *Stars* 54). Y'ang-Yeovil's Chinese roots do not extend to his appearance. He "looks" Native American, as we learn when he assumes the identity of *Vorga*'s chef assistant Angelo Poggi, one of Gully's leads: "He had put on forty pounds weight with glandular shots. He had darkened his complexion with diet manipulation. His features, never of an Oriental cast but cut more along the hawklike lines of the Ancient American Indian, easily fell into an unreliable pattern with a little muscular control" (158).

Y'ang-Yeovil is a shapeshifter whose identity can't be pinned down. Enabled by technology, he literally transforms into another man. In and of himself, Bester quantifies him as unquantifiable—he is at once Chinese and not Chinese. This is related to the "cultivated subtlety" of his cryptic ancestry, personal history, and life experience, with Bester capitalizing on stereotypes of mysterious Asian characters and Eastern mysticism. And yet Bester undermines that stereotype by simultaneously dislocating Y'ang-Yeovil from it, refusing to fully orientalize him. To some degree, he is *de*-orientalized. The fluidity of Y'ang-Yeovil's identity—physically and culturally—may be Bester's most successful gesture toward the Vanishing Point in the novel.

Overall, though, most of the characters in *Stars* are white. Stripped of the future, Gully and Presteign could just as easily serve as the protagonist and antagonist in a Dickens novel. Even the Scientific People, "the only savages of the twenty-fifth century," seem to be white (27). This brings me back to the question of racial types. By "types," I don't get the sense that Bester is referring to constructedness (i.e., racial categories as illusory). He means physical difference. Hence the other side of the Vanishing Point would look like … an Aryan utopia? That's harsh, and Bester wasn't a Nazi, of course, but given the clues and bread crumbs he leaves us, it's not totally illogical that, if nothing else, the way he perceived a futuristic, fully miscegenated society would be more white than anything else.

Then again, Bester is a master satirist, and it's not inconceivable that he's making fun of the *idea* of an all-white space-age cast by lampooning the *ideals* of Victorian culture and literature—not only with respect to race, but class and gender as well. Gully and Presteign are caricatures of white, male, socioeconomic types. Everybody in the novel is a caricature, exaggerated for pyrotechnical effect. *Stars* is a product of Bester's comic-book roots, after all. And whereas Bester is a product of his own culture, confined by architectures of psyche, power, and patriarchy, he is also an escape artist who draws lines of flight from the real-life Freak Factory that bore him.

REFERENCES

Barr, Marleen, ed. "Preface: 'All at One Point' Conveys the Point, Period; or, Black Science Fiction Is Bursting Out All Over." *Afro-Future Females: Black Writers Chart Science Fiction's Newest New Wave Trajectory.* Columbus: The Ohio State University Press, 2008. ix–xxiv.

Bester, Alfred. "Introduction: 'Oddy and Id.'" *Starlight: The Great Short Fiction of Alfred Bester.* Garden City: Nelson Doubleday, 1976.

———. "Science Fiction and the Renaissance Man." 1959. *Redemolished.* New York: iBooks, 2000.

———. *The Stars My Destination.* 1956. New York: Vintage Books, 1996.

Bier, Jesse. "The Masterpiece in Science Fiction: Power or Parody?" *Journal of Popular Culture* 12.4 (Spring 1979): 604–10.

Blackmore, Tim. "The Bester/Chaykin Connection: An Examination of Substance Assisted by Style." *Extrapolation* 31.2 (Spring 1990): 101–24.

Delany, Samuel. "The Mirror of Afrofuturism." *Extrapolation* 61.1–2 (Spring/Summer 2020): 173–84.

Douglass, Frederick. *Narrative of the Life of Frederick Douglass.* 1845. New York: W.W. Norton and Company, 2017.

Gaiman, Neil. "Of Time, and Gully Foyle." *The Stars My Destination.* New York: Vintage Books, 1996. vii–x.

Harrison, M. John. "The Rape of the Possible." *Frontier Crossings: Conspiracy '87 45th Annual World Science Fiction Convention*, edited by Robert Jackson. London: Science Fiction Conventions Ltd., 1987. 26–28.

Hipolito, Jane and Willis E. McNelly. "The Statement Is the Self: Alfred Bester's Science Fiction." *The Stellar Gauge: Essays on Science Fiction Writers*, edited by Michael J. Tolley and Kirpal Singh. Victoria: Norstrilia Press, 1980. 63–90.

Hlavaty, Arthur D. *Review of American Science Fiction: Nine Classic Novels of the 1950s*, edited by Gary K. Wolfe. *The New York Review of Science Fiction*. February 10, 2013. https://www.nyrsf.com/2013/02/american-science-fiction-nine-classic-novels-of-the-1950s-edited-by-gary-k-wolfe.html. Accessed February 8, 2021.

Kelleghan, Fiona. "*The Stars My Destination* by Alfred Bester." *The Greenwood Encyclopedia of Science Fiction*. Westport: Greenwood Publishing, 2005. 1271–73.

LaFleur, Ingrid. "Visual Aesthetics of Afrofuturism." TEDx Fort Greene Salon. *YouTube*. September 25, 2011. https://www.youtube.com/watch?v=x7bCaSzk9Zc. Accessed April 20, 2021.

Langford, David and Brian Stableford. "Psychology." *The Encyclopedia of Science Fiction*. September 29, 2020. http://www.sf-encyclopedia.com/entry/psychology. Accessed March 29, 2021.

Langford, David, Peter Nicholls, and Brian Stableford. "Race in SF." *The Encyclopedia of Science Fiction*. February 23, 2021. http://www.sf-encyclopedia.com/entry/race_in_sf. Accessed April 17, 2021.

Nietzsche, Friedrich. *Thus Spoke Zarathustra*. 1883. New York: Penguin Books, 2003.

Platt, Charles. "Attack-Escape." *New Worlds Quarterly #4*. New York: Berkley Books, 1972. 210–20.

Smith, Jad. *Alfred Bester*. Chicago: University of Illinois Press, 2016.

Vint, Sherryl. *Science Fiction*. Cambridge: The MIT Press, 2021.

Wendell, Carolyn. *Alfred Bester*. 1982. Cabin John: Wildside Press, 2006.

Womack, Ytasha L. *Afrofuturism: The World of Black Sci-Fi and Fantasy Culture*. Chicago: Lawrence Hill Books, 2013.

CHAPTER 6

Speaking in Gutter Tongues

Abstract The theme of religion pervades *Stars* and emerges in multiple ways, ranging from Cellar Christians and Gully's transformation into a deterritorialized Anti-Christ to the "blind faith" required to jaunt, the mysticism of the Scientific People, and the sensory deprived Skoptsys who live like zombified monks in the caves of Mars. Subtly or indiscreetly, Bester has something to say about religion in every chapter. In particular, Gully's lower-class gutter tongue "speaks" to his (anti)religious identity as well as the broader context of Bester's SF authorship. Both the protagonist and the author are metaphorical exorcists who aspire to "cleanse" their respective worlds—one from the violence of upper-class tyranny and prejudice, the other from the limitations of SF writers who fail to live up to the genre's great potential.

Keywords Religion · Language · Ideology · Exorcism · Violence

THE ANTI-CHRIST

At the New Year's Eve ball in Australia where Gully debuts as Geoffrey Fourmyle of Ceres, he tells Robin that he has three leads to the man responsible for leaving him to die on *Nomad*. One is *Vorga* crewman Ben

© The Author(s), under exclusive license to Springer Nature 101
Switzerland AG 2022
D. Harlan Wilson, *Alfred Bester's The Stars My Destination*,
Palgrave Science Fiction and Fantasy: A New Canon,
https://doi.org/10.1007/978-3-030-96946-2_6

Forrest. He and Robin track him down. They find him among a congregation of Cellar Christians, a cult that must worship in underground speakeasies, not to avoid persecution, but prosecution. "The twenty-fifth century had not yet abolished God, but it had abolished religion" (Bester, *Stars* 145). It's okay to believe in God—and, for that matter, to *become* God—in this future. Organized religion, however, is illegal and must be conducted in secret.

This is one of many critical gestures toward religion in *Stars*. In Palumbo's view, Cellar Christians signify a "spiritual impoverishment" that Gully aspires to repair by "assum[ing] the two-fold role of making this benighted world spiritually significant and humankind comprehensible to itself" (338, 339). And yet the world of *Stars* is already spiritually significant, enabled rather than disabled by the loss of organized religion. Gully doesn't want to make humankind comprehensible to itself by reminding everybody what has been lost. Religion should stay lost. On the road to the superhuman, Gully implores everybody to follow him, to transcend the indoctrination of Christian ideology in particular and subpoena Nietzsche's Anti-Christ, a Zarathustrian tiger whose "teaching comes out of one's own burning" (Nietzsche 184).

The mysterious Burning Man that recurs throughout the novel turns out to be Gully haphazardly leaping back and forth in space and time after Old St. Pat's Cathedral collapses on him and he catches fire in the wreckage. The extreme fear and anxiety he experiences mirrors that of Charles Fort Jaunte when he caught fire and jaunted for the first time. Gully is the next step in the evolutionary process. Jaunte teleported across a room. Gully teleports across spacetime. There is a "scientific" reason and explanation for his burning. At the same time, it symbolizes his spiritual awakening as well as the emotional volatility of his character and the trials he must endure (i.e., "one's own burning") before he comes out on the other side as a bona fide teacher, like Nietzsche the philosopher and Zarathustra the free-spirited "madman." In this anti-Christian allegory, Gully simultaneously plays and unpacks the role of Jesus. He won't die for human beings. But he will dream for them.

The theme of religion emerges in multiple ways, ranging from Cellar Christians and Gully's transformation into a deterritorialized Anti-Christ to the "blind faith" required to jaunt, the mysticism of the Scientific People, and the sensory deprived Skoptsys who live like zombified monks in the caves of Mars. Subtly or indiscreetly, Bester has something to say about religion in every chapter. I am especially interested in how the gutter tongue "speaks" to this theme in the novel and in the broader context of Bester's SF authorship. Above all, gutterspeak marks Gully as a lower-class prole, but it also operates like religion, an insignia of his "sinful" social status that consistently dictates the flows of his emotions and actions. We are what we speak as much as what we eat, and Gully's slow molting of the gutter tongue parallels his molting of all of the social and cultural constructs that made him into a Common Man. Furthermore, Bester's playful conception of the gutter tongue (among other narrative experiments) reifies the stylistic complexity and diversity of *Stars*, "sermonizing" the way for the SF avant-garde that would follow him. Gully becomes a prophet. So did *Stars* become prophetic.

"Gonna Sermonize, Me"

To convert from ordinary prole to ultraviolent tiger to transcendent übermensch, Gully walks the plank of Christian "salvation": he must confess his sins, relinquish his guilt, and reduce himself into a glutton for punishment.

In the final chapter, Gully makes a choice between himself and society. "Am I to turn PyrE over to the world and let it destroy itself? Am I to teach the world how to space-jaunte and let us spread our freak show from galaxy to galaxy through all the universe?" (Bester, *Stars* 250). He implicates Presteign, Dagenham, and Y'ang-Yeovil with himself. "The common man's been whipped and led long enough by driven men like us … Compulsive men … Tiger men who can't help lashing the world before them. We're all tigers, the three of us, but who the hell are we to make decisions for the world just because we're compulsive? […] Are we to be scapegoats for the world forever?" (254). Presteign wants PyrE so he can blow up the Outer Planets and rule the roost. This sort of egocentric power-ploy is exactly what Gully comes to despise in himself; all of his actions up to this point have been driven by self-interest. As desiring-machines, these two tigers mirror one another and represent the instinctual aggressive compulsion of all human beings. Freud discusses this compulsion in *Civilization and Its Discontents* (1930), arguing that the "human love of aggression" is a definitive characteristic that goes back to primitive times where it "reigned almost without limit" (71). An eternal recurrence of that reign afflicts the wartime culture of *Stars*, and Gully gets caught in the middle of it. His super(anti)heroic ascension is an accident.

Earlier, I suggested that Gully is a slavemaster to Robin. He also enslaves himself. Now he wants his freedom—freedom from desire, freedom from psyche, freedom from the burden of conscience. "I want to pay for what I've done and settle the account," he concedes. "I want to get rid of this damnable cross I'm carrying ... this ache that's cracking my spine. I want to go back to Gouffre Martel. I want a lobo, if I deserve it ... and I know I do" (249). Presteign, Dagenham, and Y'ang-Yeovil won't have it; they assure him that there's no escape, not from himself, not from them. Robin disagrees—"There must always be sin and forgiveness," she declares (249)—and Jiz thinks he shouldn't accept Presteign's offer for power, honor, and wealth if he hands over PyrE: "Don't accept. If you want to be a savior, destroy the secret. Don't give PyrE to anyone" (248). Gully doesn't know what to do. Appropriately, it is not a human but Presteign's robotic bartender that gives him the final push he needs to do the right thing. Eavesdropping on their conversion, the robot says: "A man is a member of society first, and an individual second. You must go along with society, whether it chooses destruction or not" (250).

Gully jaunts back to Old St. Pat's Cathedral and discovers an altar. "Two centuries before, when organized religion had been abolished and orthodox worshippers of all faiths had been driven underground, some devout souls had constructed this secret niche in Old St. Pat's and turned it into an altar. The gold of the crucifix still shone with the brilliance of eternal faith. At the foot of the cross rested a small black box of Inert Lead Isotope" (252). The box contains PyrE, and Gully thinks it's an omen. At last, he resolves to play Christ and undo his burden.

Jaunting from one world stage to the next with his "devil face glow[ing] blood red," Gully disseminates PyrE (i.e., power) to the people, delivering bits of wisdom in the gutter tongue so that the masses will understand him (253). He decides to give people knowledge, to "[s]top treating them like children. Explain the loaded gun to them. Bring it all out into the open. [...] No more secrets from now on. No more telling children what's best for them to know ... Let 'em all grow up" (254). What people do with PyrE is up to them, but at least now they have the choice. Power-hungry slavemasters like Presteign will no longer determine their fate.

Gully's last stop is Piccadilly Circus, a commercial road junction in London. Perched on the bronze head of a statue of Eros, the Greek god of love, he carps:

Listen a me, all you! Listen, man! Gonna sermonize, me. Dig this, you!
[…] You pigs, you. You rut like pigs, is all. You got the most in you,
and you use the least. You hear me, you? Got a million in you and spend
pennies. Got a genius in you and think crazies. Got a heart in you and
feel empties. All a you. Every you […] Take a war to make you spend.
Take a jam to make you think. Take a challenge to make you great. Rest
of the time you sit around lazy, you. Pigs, you! All right, God damn you!
I challenge you, me. Die or live and be great. Blow yourselves to Christ
gone or come and find me, Gully Foyle, and I make you men. I make you
great. I give you the stars. (255)

This is the longest unbroken usage of the gutter tongue in the novel. Prior
to this moment, we don't see much of the vernacular: it's talked about
more than it's actually talked. The raw, simplistic, punchy, fragmented
syntax reflects the social, emotional, and intellectual status of the so-called
Common Man, whose ability to express himself is limited by a lack of
education and the forces of culture, which are built by the social elite to
keep him down and out.

Tim Blackmore praises Bester for his expertise in wordplay. For
instance, "[u]sing his limited keyboard, Bester created &kins ('Atkins'),
Duffy Wyg&, Jo 1/4maine, Powell's three satellite esters Wyken, Blyken,
and Nod, while all the Scientific People in *Destination* have their gender
built into their names. […] This is more than slick writing; it is the
author pressing new visions on his readers" (113, 103). Bester's wordplay looks like child's play today, and compared to the linguistic boldness
of SF novels like Anthony Burgess's *A Clockwork Orange* (1962), Russell
Hoban's *Ridley Walker* (1980), and Iain M. Banks's *Feersum Endjinn*
(1994), *Stars* is a conservative, accessible, reader-friendly work. It's
certainly nothing like Joyce's *Ulysses* or *Finnegans Wake*—the two most
ambitious SF novels ever written, in my opinion—but then again, Bester
didn't aspire to usurp or complicate story with style. His experiments
are small-scale supplements to narrative. In the absence of the Scientific People's gender symbols and the fifteenth chapter's typography and
imagery, almost nothing is lost, and the book still would have been just
as successful. Similarly, Bester's execution of the gutter tongue could be
enhanced, but he didn't have a lot of leeway.

If *Stars* had been written a decade or two later, gutterspeak might look
quite different. Composed in the twenty-first century, I'd expect it to be
riddled with expletives, and if Bester were aspiring for absolute realism,

expletives would likely dwarf all other verbiage, exemplifying gutters-peak's inherent anger, animosity, illiteracy, violence, and pathology. But the limitations of the Common Man extend to his author, who couldn't fully express himself without censorship (and possibly prosecution) for obscenity. Bester still pushed the bill. Five years before the publication of *Stars*, J. D. Salinger's *The Catcher in the Rye* (1951) came out. The novel was widely banned for language and sexuality despite an absence of explicit sex (by today's standards, anyway) and "extremist" taboo terms like *shit* and *fuck*. *Goddamn* was the catalyst, and Bester uses it aplenty, but he got away with it, partly because Holden Caulfield is a kid and Gully is a man, partly because *Catcher* is set in a realistic, relatable present whereas *Stars* unfolds in a surreal, estranging future. God-fearing readers could forgive Bester, but not Salinger, whose style and storyline hit too close to home.

The gutter tongue's diminutive lexicon emboldens the undereducated identity of its speaker. Bester strips language to the bone and formulates a dialogue of clipped utterances and verbal stabs. In lieu of expletives, he condenses and sometimes inverts syntax, rendering an assertion like "All a you fuckin' shitheads're motherfuckin' pigs" as "You pigs, you." As in this instance, he frequently ends sentences with a reiteration of an object pronoun (i.e., "me" or "you"). This is similar to the way in which people use "dude," "like," or "nah mean" today (e.g., "Dude, I'm, like, angry I'm a prole, nah mean?"). It's an incessant crutch-word, a rhetorical anchor used by people who have not developed the skills or vocabulary to articulate themselves, and it can turn into a habit. For Gully, "Gonna sermonize, me" (i.e., "I am going to deliver a sermon to you") epitomizes how the gutter tongue compresses and rearranges dialogue, objectifying the subject pronoun ("I") at the end of the utterance. The construction of this particular utterance also incriminates the speaker. Gully isn't just delivering a sermon to the masses. He's punctuating the fact that he ("me") is the voice of the sermon. An important part of his demolition/reconstruction is the manifestation of an authentic, genuine voice that belongs to him. The gutter tongue was imprinted upon him by the culture machine. Now he's making it his own. Now he's *Making It New*.

As much as Gully wants to help people help themselves, he wants them to see him for who he really is. The subtext of his me-sermon is the very subtext that flares up on his face when his emotions escape him—*I am a tiger: hear me roar*—only now he knows how to control and channel it.

He has learned to be his own circus tamer. He wants humanity to recognize his accomplishment, and he wants everybody to do likewise (i.e., *to become what he has become*) in the interest of creating a better, gentler world. There is a self-referentiality to gutterspeak that marks Gully like stigmata. His climactic world tour of sermons is a self-induced exorcism as well as a fusillade of enlightenment.

The gutter tongue operates something like Pentecostal tongues. Pentecostalism is a subdivision of Christianity that centers on the Holy Spirit and the idea that God exists in the body of the believer. In Christianity, the Holy Spirit (or Holy Ghost) belongs to a trinity of coeternal, consubstantial figures, the other two being "the Father" (God) and "the Son" (Jesus). All three figures are versions of God who play different roles. The Holy Spirit serves as a mediator between the Father and the Son, the latter of whom is a stand-in for humanity. In the New Testament's Book of Acts, the day of the Pentecost occurs when the Holy Spirit descends on the apostles of Jesus and floods their sensoria. As a result, they explode with uncontrollable xenoglossy: "And suddenly there came a sound from heaven as of a rushing mighty wind, and it filled all the house where they were sitting. And there appeared unto them cloven tongues as of fire, and it sat upon each of them. And they were all filled with the Holy Ghost, and began to speak with other tongues, as the Spirit gave them utterance" (Acts 245). This charism empowers speakers as supernatural "children" of God; with the spiritual gift of glossolalia, they are enabled to execute the mission of the church, the home of God's Word on earth.

In and of itself, the gutter tongue isn't spiritual, but like the Pentecost's "cloven tongues of fire" (perfect for Gully), it's a nonsense language through which the god of culture "speaks" its speaker. God isn't dead in *Stars*, but he's moribund, and Gully sets himself up for becoming a new god, one who is not Christian (or affiliated with any organized religion) but who remains invested in the greater good.

Following his sermons, Gully jaunts beyond spacetime "to an Elsewhere and an Elsewhen. He arrived in chaos. He hung for a moment and then tumbled back into chaos […], a burning spear flung from unknown into unknown" (Bester, *Stars* 255–56). In this paranormal, pathological void, he has a brief internal dialogue with himself. These are the last words he utters in the novel, communicated in plain English now:

"*I believe*," he thought. "*I have faith.*"
"*Faith in what?*" he asked himself, adrift in limbo.

"Faith in faith," he answered himself. *"It isn't necessary to have something to believe in. It's only necessary to believe that somewhere there's something worthy of belief."* (256)

Gully's rise to godliness annuls God; all that matters is ideology itself, or rather, *an ideology of the self*, the belief in the vast potential of the individual freed from the hammer of social and cultural construction. Together such individuals could make a great society. Gully articulates this epiphany shortly before returning to *Nomad*'s womb-locker to be reborn. In Piccadilly Circus, his last usage of the gutter tongue, a language of *ignorance*, paradoxically disseminates *knowledge*. This paradox is exacerbated by the contrast between his text and his image. Like Jesus, he teaches people how to be good shepherds—but with his mask ablaze, he looks like the Devil. In Gully, Christ and Anti-Christ bleed together, and by deconstructing himself, he deconstructs the residua of this binary Christian power structure. By the time he enunciates his final words, he has moved beyond the gutter tongue, a "damnable cross" shrugged off of his shoulders once and for all.

SKOPTSYS AND CELLAR CHRISTIANS

In the interval between his last words and return to *Nomad*, Gully jaunts across the universe, pausing on five occasions at different stars: Rigel, Vega, Canopus, Aldebaran, and Antares—all the brightest stars in the constellations of, respectively, Orion, Lyra, Carina, Taurus, and Scorpius. This narrative constellation of flash-scenes makes the novel's title a reality as Gully bears witness to the spacetime continuum in all of its glory.

Near Rigel, "Foyle hung, freezing and suffocating in space, face to face with the incredible destiny in which he believed, but which was still inconceivable. He hung in space for a blinding moment, as helpless, as amazed, and yet as inevitable as the first gilled creature to come out of the sea and hang gulping on a primeval beach in the dawn-history of life on earth" (256). Near Canopus, he becomes that gilled creature, "gulping on the beach of the universe, nearer death than life, nearer the future than the past" (257). Everything implodes into Gully, who is everything that ever was, is, and will be—the biblical Alpha and Omega. Gully's id has been suppressed, and his ego has merged with the cosmos. His solar identity illuminates mankind's connection to the universe, and vice versa, from the smallest molecules to the largest supernovas. *Stars* concludes on this pantheistic note. Belief is important, says the novel. God, however, is only as important as our ability to find a higher power within ourselves and recognize that we are all part of spatial and temporal eternity. As such, we are responsible for taking care of ourselves, not killing ourselves.

Bester paves the road to this thesis with the asphalt of Gully's experience and evolution. He introduces the idea of blind faith in the prologue when he recounts the history of the Jaunte Age. In order to jaunte, one must *believe* in one's ability to do it. "The slightest doubt would block the mind-thrust necessary for teleportation," just as doubt in the idea that Jesus is a messiah who died for humanity's sins might "block" one's admittance into Heaven (11). And an excess of doubt might land a disbeliever in Hell, which is where Gully finds himself in the rubble of Old St. Pat's, burning and bereft, before rising from the flames, shooting to the stars, and becoming a shooting star himself. Ideology and the notion of faith is thus knitted into the fabric of everyday life. Without it, life won't work anymore. Jaunting has revolutionized civilization and brought about a communal dependency on its constant enaction.

Religion may be outlawed in *Stars*, but there are traces of it everywhere. In the first chapter, we learn that Gully "wasted no time on prayer or thanks but continued the business of survival," indicating that divine supplication still exists in some form, and he may have "wasted time" on it in the past (19). Elsewhere, we learn that standard modes of religion have been sublimated into other areas, such as the nurturing of Martian nature:

> After two centuries of colonization, the air struggle on Mars was still so critical that the V-L Law, the Vegetative-Lynch Law, was still in effect. It was a killing offense to endanger or destroy any plant vital to the transformation of Mars' carbon dioxide atmosphere into an oxygen atmosphere. Even blades of grass were sacred. There was no need to erect KEEP OFF THE GRASS neons. The man who wandered off a path onto a lawn would be instantly shot. The woman who picked a flower would be killed without mercy. Two centuries of sudden death had inspired a reverence for green growing things that almost amounted to a religion. (198)

Regarding language, at one point Robin calls out Gully for his unknowing use of religiously charged rhetoric:

> "Did you ever stop to think what swearing is?" Robin asked quietly.
> "You say 'Jesus' and 'Jesus Christ.' Do you know what that is?"

"Just swearing, that's all. Like 'ouch' or 'damn.'"

"No, it's religion. You don't know it, but there are two thousand years of meaning behind words like that."

"This is not time for dirty talk," Foyle said impatiently. (145)

Robin isn't critiquing Gully for using God's name in vain. That would be silly: as Gully indicates, religion itself (and everything it entails) amounts to "dirty talk." Instead, she tries to explain how the ghost of religion still haunts twenty-fifth-century discourse.

Most noticeably, Bester depicts the ghost of religion via two groups of deviants: Skoptsys and Cellar Christians. In both cases, he associates their deviance with sexuality.

Gully's quest to find out who gave the order for *Vorga* to bypass *Nomad* takes a long time as he steps on and over numerous leads to the truth. He's our lens: we know what he knows, and as he gathers clues and puts the pieces of the puzzle together, so do readers. Eventually, he discovers that *Vorga* had been smuggling war refugees away from Callisto and the Outer Planets. Rather than bring the refugees to safety, the captain of the ship, Lindsey Joyce, confiscated their belongings, then dumped them into space, like Nazis plundering Jews and sending them to the gas chamber. Not until later does Gully realize that Olivia orchestrated the subterfuge (and his collateral abandonment) as part of her battle against humanity. At first, though, he thinks the blame lies with Joyce.

Guilt-ridden from her crimes, Joyce becomes a Skoptsy and retreats to a colony on Mars. Bester extrapolates Skoptsys from a sect of Russian Orthodox Christians that formed in the eighteenth century. Gully calls these monastic zombies "the living dead" (200). Not only do they practice abstinence, they literally cut ties with all of their senses: "The ancient Skoptsy sect of White Russia, believing that sex was the root of all evil, practiced an atrocious self-castration to extirpate the root. The modern Skoptsys, believing that sensation was the root of all evil, practiced an even more barbaric custom. Having entered the Skoptsy Colony and paid a fortune for the privilege, the initiates submitted joyously to an operation that severed the sensory nervous system, and lived out their days without sight, sound, speech, smell, taste, or touch" (ibid.). They exist in the darkness of underground catacombs, without social interaction, and with just enough sustenance and exercise to stay alive. The main purpose of such an existence is to purify the mind and body of original sin, which lives in the senses. For Joyce, it's penance for mass murder.

Gully doesn't just show up on Mars and find Joyce. As always, he must find somebody else to lead the way to his next lead. Here it's the only fully operational Martian telepath, Sigurd Magsman, "an ancient, ancient child" who possesses as much wisdom as he does immaturity (199). In fact, he's a spoiled brat, kowtowed by everybody on the planet. Gully kidnaps him, forces him to do his bidding. At the Skoptsy monastery, they discover Joyce among her flock, all of them "white as slugs, mute as corpses, motionless as Buddhas" (201). Gully didn't know Joyce is a woman; because of purdah, she had to masquerade as a man in order to climb the officer ranks. He's doubly taken aback when the Burning Man shows up and reveals that Olivia, not Joyce, was the one who gave the bypass order. All along, he thought that men had been in charge of his demolition, but it was two women, one of which he loves dearly.

There is a Buddhist component to Bester's Skoptsys, who acknowledge suffering and practice a kind of mindfulness, yet as Sigurd tells Gully, "[t]hey're sick … all sick … like worms in their heads" (201). Nirvana doesn't await them; they each live in their own personal, pathological Hell. For the most part, their ideological roots are in Christianity, the dominant ex-religion in *Stars*. Bester almost exclusively projects Western civilization and culture into the future. Anything non-occidental is incidental.

The term *skoptsky* derives from the antiquated Russian *oskopit*, which means "to castrate." Oleg Skripnik explains that "[r]itual self-castration was observed among ardent Christians long before the appearance of the sect [in the eighteenth century]. The most important tenet of the Skoptic faith, which inspired ancient Christian theologian and ascetic Origen to castrate himself, came from a passage in the Gospel according to Matthew: 'There are castrates who were castrated by others and there are castrates who castrated themselves for the Kingdom of God.'" Over time, sectarians began to interpret parts of the Bible to suit their beliefs (e.g., the idea that Jesus castrated his disciples after washing their feet).

In *Stars*, the very existence of Skoptsys threatens the phallus that Gully so vehemently embodies as an aggressive alpha male. Coupled with the discovery that Joyce is a woman and Olivia forsakened him, Gully experiences emasculation and symbolic castration on multiple levels. His fear is palpable, and it's telling that Bester poses him like Christ on the cross when he attempts to escape Mars. He's on the lam—and on the *lamb* (of

God)—for snatching Sigurd. As commandos close in on the monastery and he hastens to the nearest jaunte stage, the Outer Satellites bomb the planet. He scurries to his ship and takes off, but he's in acceleration mode, and the gravitational force throws him onto the back wall of the cockpit: "The wall appeared, to his accelerated senses, to approach him. He thrust out both arms, palms flat against the wall to brace himself. The sluggish power thrusting him back split his arms apart and forced him against the wall, gently at first, then harder and harder until face, jaw, chest, and body were crushed against the metal" (Bester, *Stars* 206). It's as if Gully has been nailed there. Once again, Bester christens him as Christ. He has risen from the catacombs of "the living dead" and blasted off of Mars. Soon he will rise from the symbolic death of his tiger-self and blast off to the stars.

In addition to foreshadowing Gully's rebirth, Skoptskys foreshadow his movement beyond the gutter tongue and language in general. They do not appear to have a voice, or at least one that we can hear, tele-pathically or actually. To extract intel from Joyce, Gully uses Sigurd, who doesn't want to look inside her head. He's afraid—it's too painful and chaotic in there, and he can't understand her. At no point does Joyce speak or give up any information. Gully gives himself the information about Olivia in the form of the Burning Man. Joyce's voicelessness is part of her punishment, one of many stigmata removed from her being. Gully's voicelessness connotes a removal of stigmata as well, but unlike Joyce's, it's only temporary. As J♂seph tells M♀ira in the last scene, he will unlock a new voice from the womb-locker in which he sleeps and dreams: "Presently he will awaken and read to us, his people, his thoughts" (258).

Cellar Christians are a counterpoint to Skoptsys. Their closet gath-erings are more like orgies than funeraries, and Bester links them to pornography and drugs.

On several occasions, characters mention Cellar Christians, never in a positive light. For example, when the specters of guilt and conscience first begin to distress Gully, he worries that he might be "turning into a white-livered Cellar Christian turning the other cheek and whining forgiveness" (195); and when Y'ang-Yeovil (disguised as Angelo Poggi) tries to bag and tag Gully on the Spanish Stairs, he pretends to be a black-market panhandler: "Filthy pictures, signore? Cellar Christians, kneeling, praying, singing psalms, kissing cross? Very naughty. Very smutty, signore. Enter-tain your friends … Excite the ladies" (158). Christianity, a forbidden fruit, has usurped sexuality as the dominant mode of porn, although sexuality remains part of the scopophilic thrill. There's still a desire for Christianity, but not like there used to be.

Gully and Robin encounter a congregation of Cellar Christians on their hunt for Ben Forrest, whose house turns out to be a conventicle. Among the congregation, Gully sees "a priest and a rabbi," insinuating that Judaism has been lumped together with this underground cult. He and Robin don't find Forrest in the basement. He's upstairs, in the attic, doing drugs. Forrest is a "twitch" who takes Analogue, a hallucinogenic that reverts him to a primal state wherein he identifies with a specific animal. Not coincidentally, "Forrest was queer for snakes," the animal most disparaged and feared in Christian lore, especially in the Old Testament's Book of Genesis, where Satan tempts Adam and Eve in the form of a serpent, robbing mankind of the bliss of ignorance (147).

There is no evidence that worshipping Cellar Christians have taken Analogue, too, but the juxtaposition of "[r]eligion in the cellar and dope upstairs" is enough (144). By associating Cellar Christians with porn and drugs, Bester accentuates the illicit status of religion in *Stars*. What used to be widely valued by the masses is now a source of contempt, weakness, and absurdity. But why? We are never told outright. Historically, nothing conceived of by the human mind is responsible for more anxiety, enmity, bloodshed, pain, and suffering than religion, but getting rid of religion didn't get rid of war and meaningless death in this imagined future. We must look to Gully for the reason. His transformation into an übermensch explains what happened to religion and why the journey away from it has been so rocky: the slow replacement of myth with mankind. Post-*Stars*, Bester implies, Gully will teach people to believe in themselves and the universe rather than harmful superstitions.

Whatever one believes, the prospect of death and nothingness is sufficiently frightening to induce the mass pathology of religion and the belief in an afterlife, a skygod, an oven in the dirt, messiahs, cosmic energy, regeneration, thetans, flying spaghetti monsters, and so on, but if the waning of religious fervor in the twentieth century is any indicator, by the twenty-fifth century, religion will be seriously marginalized. Cellar Christians could be Bester's most realistic extrapolation in *Stars*.

LAST RITES

In *The Gospel According to Science Fiction* (2007), Gabriel Mckee makes a case for the religious tenor of SF, refuting the idea that the genre downplays religion and is atheistic, if only by prioritizing science and technology over spirituality. The book was printed by Presbyterian publisher Westminister John Knox Press, and McKee's unease and insecurity about the genre (or anything) not being religious comes across in spades. The same can be said for his blog, *SF Gospel*, and the entry he writes on *Stars*, "'Cellar Christians': What It Really Means When an SF Author Says Religion Doesn't Exist in the Future." Responding to other bloggers who assume that SF and religion don't mix, he uses *Stars* to show that even SF texts in which religion has been outlawed are religious at their core. "In *The Stars My Destination*," he writes, "religion has been suppressed, but it *cannot* be destroyed. Indeed, by presenting religion with the terminology of pornography, Bester places the spiritual drive on a primal level equal to that of the sexual drive. By the time he introduces the Skoptsys [...], it's far more reasonable to conclude that Bester thinks human beings *must* be religious, even if his protagonist is not."

McKee is right about Bester presenting religion in terms of porn and sexuality rather than spiritual drives, but he's dead wrong about Bester's attitude toward religion as represented in the novel. What McKee fears is the absence of religion, namely Christianity—in this text or any text—and as with most devout Christians, what he wants is an endorsement of his beliefs; like the classic Skoptsy, he feels compelled to interpret *Stars* so that it suits his own needs and desires. In fact, the novel does not say that humans must be religious. It says we must have faith in our ability to become the best we can be *without God*, the idea of which has produced illimitable death and destruction throughout history. If anything, belief in science is what the novel wants, because advances in technology will allow human beings to increasingly unlock their full potential. Science, not God, is the gateway to the "new frontiers" that the Romantics cry for in the prologue. Both rely on the power of the imagination, but *Stars* thinks human beings *must not* be religious.

Langford and Stableford say that most SF definitions tend to dissociate religion from the genre, but "many of the roots of proto-SF are embedded in traditions of speculative fiction closely associated with the religious imagination, and contemporary SF recovered a strong interest in certain mystical and transcendental themes and images when it moved beyond the taboos imposed by the pulp magazines." Bester breaks these taboos not only by thematizing religion, but by making it taboo.

Stars can be read as one long exorcism. Gully is his own exorcist, but he has a lot of help, and J♂seph the priest initiates and clinches the removal of his figurative demons, setting him up to remove the demons of society at large. This reading of the novel extends to Bester's authorship. *Stars* is a meta-exorcism of the SF genre, which was possessed by the demons of pulp ethics and aesthetics. Recall Bester's thesis in "A Diatribe Against Science Fiction" that the genre "is written by empty people who have failed as human beings. As a class they are lazy, irresponsible, immature. They are incapable of producing contemporary fiction because they know nothing about life, cannot reflect life, and have no adult comment to make about life. They are silly childish people who have taken refuge in science fiction where they can establish their own arbitrary rules about reality to suit their own inadequacy" (434). He lowers the boom just as hard in "Science Fiction and the Renaissance Man," bashing the genre's inability to escape from the pulp roots planted by Hugo Gernsback:

> Gernsback broke in a half dozen writers who were maladroits as fiction writers but mature experts in one aspect of popular science or another. […] Within five years science fiction exhausted the reprint field and the prefabricated concepts, and, alas, fell into the hands of the pulp writers. It was then that the great decline set in because science fiction began to reflect the inwardness of the hack writer, and the essence of the hack writer is that he has no inwardness. He has no contact with reality, no sense of dramatic proportion, no principles of human behavior, no eye for truth … and a wooden ear for dialogue. He is all compromise and clever-shabby tricks … [S]cience fiction wallowed in this pigsty. (410, 413)

Bester and Gully are both exorcists, then, frustrated by the demons of history, fighting to elevate their respective worlds of wonder.

REFERENCES

Acts 2: 2–4. *The English Bible: King James Version*. New York: W.W. Norton and Company, 2012.

Bester, Alfred. "A Diatribe Against Science Fiction." 1961. *Redemolished*. New York: iBooks, 2000. 431–35.

———. "Science Fiction and the Renaissance Man." 1959. *Redemolished*. New York: iBooks, 2000. 408–30.

————. *The Stars My Destination*. 1956. New York: Vintage Books, 1996.

Blackmore, Tim. "The Bester/Chaykin Connection: An Examination of Substance Assisted by Style." *Extrapolation* 31.2 (Spring 1990): 101–24.

Freud, Sigmund. *Civilization and Its Discontents*. 1930. New York: W.W. Norton and Company, 1961.

Langford, David and Brian Stableford. "Religion." *The Encyclopedia of Science Fiction*. January 16, 2021. http://www.sf-encyclopedia.com/entry/psycho logy. Accessed May 3, 2021.

McKee, Gabriel. "'Cellar Christians': What It Really Means When an SF Author Says Religion Doesn't Exist in the Future." *SF Gospel*. June 4, 2008. https://sfgospel.typepad.com/sf_gospel/2008/06/cellar-christians-what-it-really-means-when-an-sf-author-says-religion-doesnt-exist-in-the-future.html. Accessed May 3, 2021.

Nietzsche, Friedrich. *The Anti-Christ*. 1895. New York: Penguin Books, 1990.

Palumbo, Donald. "The Monomyth in Alfred Bester's *The Stars My Destination*." *The Journal of Popular Culture* 38.2 (2004): 333–68.

Skripnik, Oleg. "The Skoptsy: The Story of the Russian Sect that Maimed for Its Beliefs." *Russia Beyond*. August 25, 2016. https://www.rbth.com/politics_and_society/2016/08/25/the-skoptsy-the-story-of-the-russian-sect-that-mai med-for-its-beliefs_624175. Accessed May 1, 2021.

CHAPTER 7

Coda

Abstract Just as Bester critiqued SF, so did SF critics critique Bester. Nonetheless, he remains a singular, vital author, and *Stars* is a beacon of innovation and inspiration in the SF megatext. The novel signaled the beginning of a new trend. Now it stands as a tombstone looming over the genre's resting place in the graveyard of the twentieth century.

Keyword Genre · Authorship · Innovation

I was introduced to the study of SF by Robert Crossley, an emeritus English professor at the University of Massachusetts-Boston, where I completed a M.A. degree in the mid-1990s. During my first semester, I took a course with Bob on apocalyptic literature. I had almost exclusively studied medieval, Renaissance, and Victorian literature in college, and I didn't know that something like SF studies existed. Needless to say, I loved it, and Bob became my mentor. The next semester, I took an independent study with him, and he gave me a list of important SF novels to read. Among them were William Gibson's *Neuromancer*, H. G. Wells's *The War of the Worlds*, Ursula K. Le Guin's *The Left Hand of Darkness* (1969), Octavia Butler's *Kindred* (1979), Olaf Stapledon's *Last and First Men* (1930), and last but not least, Alfred Bester's *The Stars*

© The Author(s), under exclusive license to Springer Nature
Switzerland AG 2022
D. Harlan Wilson, *Alfred Bester's The Stars My Destination*,
Palgrave Science Fiction and Fantasy: A New Canon,
https://doi.org/10.1007/978-3-030-96946-2_7

My Destination. I ate them up. All I really knew was Chaucer, Shake-speare, and Dickens, and these SF authors unlocked doorways to new and exciting realms of the imagination for me. In addition to a literary critic, I was an aspiring novelist and screenwriter, and I became so excited about *Stars* that I took it upon myself to adapt the novel into a screenplay. I didn't know what I was doing. I bought a bunch of screenplays at Tower Records and figured I would just use them as templates for my own Big Idea. My naiveté and ignorance about writing *anything* belonged to a stereotype Common Man. But something about *Stars* stirred me beyond my capacity to understand it. If nothing else, I knew this book was special.

Bester made no bones about his thoughts on the SF genre and the writers, editors, and publishers involved with it; few authors rival his outspokenness. As a matter of course, critics have been outspoken about him. One is Jesse Bier, who I cite periodically throughout this study, and who discounts Bester's contribution to SF in his 1979 article "The Masterpiece in Science Fiction: Power or Parody?":

> Writing in a genre that is really old-fashioned by now and probably, if the distinction means anything, exhausted rather than blocked, the science fictioner resorts to a series of unconscious parodies. Down deep, I suspect, he both knows and does not know his full circumstance. I rather think that Bester, in particular, knows or senses more than most of his colleagues. They may be the chief reason to consider or reconsider him as exceptional in his work, though not exactly as "apotheosis." Then again, maybe he is—since he yields up his compromised state of mind so clearly. But we ought not exalt that state of mind out of all recognition—dignifying the comic and self-parodying contradictions, the irresolutions, the overt and coded borrowings, and the final relative failure as either true art or the work of genius. In any case, it is not anywhere near "greatness." That kind of success and celebration we must reserve for far more decisive—we might as well add, profound—talent. (609)

There is some truth to what Bier says here. His final sentiments irk me. "Greatness" is a strong, subjective word, and I think "genius" is a myth, but it's absurd to suggest that Bester's contribution was neither decisive nor talented. For all of its flaws, *Stars* remains an essential touchstone for authors today. In my own writerly circles, Bester's name comes up on a regular basis, unprovoked by my admittedly excessive enthusiasm. *Stars* almost single-handedly instilled the desire in me to become a writer and a scholar of a certain disposition. I like the idea that it made me into a kind of tiger, just as it had a hand (or a claw) in making many other writers, thinkers, and artists into tigers, especially those associated with the New Wave and cyberpunk movements.

Bier's critique hinges on his belief that *Stars* is more mimetic than original. Charles Platt offers this counter-argument: *Stars* "is probably the best science fiction of its kind ever written; by definition, this also means that it is the best that ever will be written, for the worth of such science fiction lies in its ideas, and the number of possible new ideas within the self-imposed strictures of the field really is limited. *The Stars My Destination* is a summation of what had been so far achieved ... After it, everything seems at least a little derivative" (211). This assertion is a bit melodramatic. It's much closer to the truth, though.

SF may be exhausted, but what the author of *Stars* accomplished in his magnum opus defies that exhaustion. Unlike the majority of literature in any genre, the novel is a testimony to Bester's innovative prowess and the imaginative potential that most SF has failed to put into effect. It shows us how SF is at once the genre of invention, the genre of irony, and the genre of stagnation.

References

Bier, Jesse. "The Masterpiece in Science Fiction: Power or Parody?" *Journal of Popular Culture* 12.4 (Spring 1979): 604–10.

Platt, Charles. "Attack-Escape." *New Worlds Quarterly #4*. New York: Berkley Books, 1972. 210–20.

Index

© The Author(s), under exclusive license to Springer Nature Switzerland AG 2022
D. Harlan Wilson, *Alfred Bester's The Stars My Destination*, Palgrave Science Fiction and Fantasy: A New Canon, https://doi.org/10.1007/978-3-030-96946-2

Printed by Printforce, the Netherlands